# THE EAST END MURDERS
## Death By Drowning

No one saw the girl's body for a while. Then a man walking his bike along the path saw what he thought was a doll's head, face down in the water. The hair was a mix of colours, blonde with bright red clumps, some darker hair at the roots. He'd passed by at first, but then backed up a few paces.

She was pulled out of the freezing water and laid on her side. A young girl of about sixteen, her face the colour of cement, her mouth open, some of the dirty river water trickling out of it down her cheek. Behind, at waist level, her hands were tied together with deep pink ribbon; yards of it layered around her wrists and topped off with a bow.

POINT CRIME

# THE EAST END MURDERS

## Death By Drowning

**Anne Cassidy**

SCHOLASTIC

Scholastic Children's Books,
Commonwealth House, 1-19 New Oxford Street,
London WC1A 1NU, UK
a division of Scholastic Ltd
London ~ New York ~ Toronto ~ Sydney ~ Auckland
Mexico City ~ New Delhi ~ Hong Kong

First published in the UK by Scholastic Ltd., 1999

ISBN 0 439 01057 8

Typeset by TW Typesetting, Midsomer Norton, Somerset
Printed by Cox and Wyman Ltd, Reading, Berks.

10 9 8 7 6 5 4 3 2 1

# Contents

# 1

# The River

In winter months, the river Lea was a grim water-way that crept dismally through the back of north London, curling past silent factories and roaring dual carriageways. Its dark brown water seemed dense, almost solid. It had a lifeless look about it, as if it were generations since any creature had swum there. From place to place there was a hopeful boy or man fishing, their rods dipping into the soupy water, their boxes of squirming maggots lying open by their feet.

In February, on the day after Valentine's Day, it was raw and cold, the mud on the path crisp underfoot. The water was dotted with silvery patches of ice that shone in between the bottles and bits of old furniture and Coke cans that bobbed up and down like a flotilla.

No one saw the girl's body for a while. The police report said that it must have been partially hidden by some old tarpaulin that had fallen off one of the barges that sometimes came along. A man had been walking his bike along a narrow stretch of the path when he saw what he thought was a doll's head, face down in the water. The hair was a mix of colours, blonde with bright red clumps, some darker hair at the roots. He'd passed by at first, but then backed up a few paces.

The police came in a car, their wheels slipping over the icy ground. They'd had to use long dredging poles to pull her into the side, the debris around her moving clumsily along as well. When they realized it was a body they'd gone back to their radios and called for another team. *We weren't properly equipped,* they'd said in their report.

She was pulled out of the freezing water about an hour later and laid on her side. The photos were taken from several angles. A young girl of about sixteen, her face the colour of cement, her mouth open, some of the dirty river water trickling out of it down her cheek. Behind, at waist level, her hands were tied together with deep pink ribbon; yards of it layered around her wrists and topped off with a bow of sorts.

Later, they found out that her name was Susan Yorke. She'd been a drifter and had lived here and there among the dozens of young, homeless people who hung around the area. There were reports in the newspapers for a few days. I remembered reading a couple of them. She'd had alcohol in her bloodstream and there'd been talk of parties in disused factories along the river. One of the local newspapers had hinted at games of "Dare" and had coined the heading: *DEADLY DARE, Did Teenager Die in Children's Game Tragedy?* The interest didn't last though. Some local government scandal knocked it off the front page.

Susan Yorke's death only made ripples for a few days and then sank quietly without a trace. Her death had been written up in some policeman's file and then put away. Just another homeless kid who'd got herself into trouble.

There was every chance that she'd have been forgotten about completely, except that on March 15th, a month later, another young girl's body was found in the same stretch of the river Lea. Her name was Jennifer Ryan and she was almost seventeen, a student at a local sixth-form college.

She had drowned and her hands had been tied together with ribbon.

The discovery was made by two young boys who were trying out a metal detector along the river bank. It was an early spring day, the sky a cobalt blue, the river bank yellow with wild daffodils. She'd been found at a place where the river widened and the sides were thick with reeds. She must have floated along and got caught in the bend, face down, her legs floating out behind her, looking like someone snorkelling. She had a blonde ponytail and it had fanned out on top of the grimy water, its ends curling neatly.

The police had come quickly, their wheels tearing up the muddy ground, their lights blinking. This time there'd been three squad cars as well as the ambulance, the scene-of-crime officers and the pathologist. A police officer that I knew had told me that the river bank had been crowded out, people squeezing past each other, scouring the ground for clues, their faces grim.

Her body was pulled out with great care. She came up slowly, helped from the water by a diver in a black wetsuit who said afterwards that she'd seemed weightless, like a small child. She lay half on her back while the police stood glumly around her. Her face had been pretty; her hair hung like wet straw on one shoulder. She'd had a short, sparkly dress on, the type you might wear to go out somewhere special. Her hands had been pulled behind her back, the ribbon wound around over and over, and then tied in a bow. The police officer I knew said that she'd looked like a grisly Barbie doll, wrapped up and ready to be given as a present.

Susan Yorke and Jennifer Ryan, both fished out of an otherwise dead river, both with their hands tied behind them with fancy pink ribbon. The police had stopped talking about games of "Dare" and started looking for a killer.

I hadn't known much about it at the time. I'd been involved in other cases but it had stuck in my mind all the same. A year later, though, I'd read a newspaper article that had brought it all back.

I'd been sitting in the kitchen at my boyfriend's house. On the table between us was the Valentine's card he had sent me. On it he'd written, *To Patsy, all my love, Billy*. I'd felt a bit embarrassed because I hadn't bought him one, hadn't thought that it would be the kind of thing he would like. Instead of apologizing, I'd taken an offensive line.

"You're not supposed to write your name in these!" I said.

"I'll remember next time," Billy said, flicking through a car magazine. He was looking unconcerned, as if he wasn't really listening to me. A lot of people we knew said that we often seemed like a couple who had been married for donkey's years. The truth was we'd just known each other for a very long time.

"And you're not supposed to send them to someone you've been seeing for a while!" I said, trying to justify myself.

"What are they for then?" he said, lazily, not really bothered.

"They're for people who like each other but haven't yet got it off the ground."

"You make it sound like a hot-air balloon."

"You know what I mean. They haven't started going out together."

"I don't remember you sending me one last year," he said. He was referring to the long period when we'd been just friends before we'd both had the courage to admit our feelings about each other.

"I…I can't remember. I thought I had sent you one," I said.

"Patsy, it's one thing to try and make excuses but don't tell lies!"

I sat silently and caught his smile of victory.

"Cup of tea?" he said, and I nodded in a sort of defeated way. I had forgotten to send him a Valentine's card and there was no excuse I could make. I picked up the nearby newspaper, gave it a shake and pretended to be absorbed in it.

The article was tiny, a small block of print at the bottom of page four.

### RIVER LEA MURDERS: ONE YEAR ON

*Police sources say they are still no nearer finding the killer of the two girls who were pulled out of the river Lea just one year ago. The girls' distinctively bound hands led to the incident being nicknamed the Gift-wrap Murders.*

*At the time, many hundreds of police hours were spent tracking down clues and interviewing local residents. It was feared that a serial killer could be on the loose and the police waited, fearful of more deaths. No other such cases were reported and police were left looking for the link between the two girls in the hope that this might lead them to the callous murderer.*

*Senior police officer Heather Warren said yesterday, "It is true to say that police inquiries on this matter have been scaled down. However, the file is still open and on this, the anniversary of the first death, the police would welcome any information from the public which might give a lead on this heinous crime."*

I shook my head, remembering the case. Two young girls pulled out of the water like dead fish.

"What's the matter?" Billy said.

"Nothing," I said, "just a story in the paper."

"Not more death and destruction," he said dismissively, handing me a cup of steaming tea. He took the newspaper off me and started to read it.

It was a complaint he had been making about me for a while. According to him, I was always poring over stories about murder or accounts of freak accidents. I denied it loudly but inside I knew he was right. I had become fascinated with the randomness of death and the way people, like toys, were just snatched up and thrown out of the game for no other reason than they were in the wrong place at the wrong time. Truthfully, it depressed me.

Don't get me wrong, I wasn't obsessed by death. It wasn't as if I hadn't come into contact with it in the previous eighteen months. Since working at my uncle's detective agency I'd been involved in a number of murder investigations, a couple of them just as unpleasant as the river Lea murders. I'd met parents of murdered teenagers and I'd even seen a couple of ghastly white bodies, cold to the touch, their faces etched with their last expression, their final moments alive.

I'd been lucky in those cases, often wandering in circles for days before the pieces of the crime began to join together. From time to time I'd got myself into danger, I'd ignored advice and gone after people on my own. Somehow, though, I'd come out of it OK. That's what I couldn't understand. Here I was, rubbing shoulder to shoulder with people who had committed murder and I was all right. Yet someone's mother or son could get into a car, drive to the local supermarket and get hit by a juggernaut that had taken a wrong turn and was hurrying to get back on track. The wrong place at the wrong time.

It was like a lottery. That's what frightened me about death.

"I see they never found anyone for the river Lea murders." Billy's voice broke my train of thought.

"No," I said, picking up Billy's Valentine's card. *To Patsy, all my love, Billy.*

It didn't do to dwell on it.

# 2
# The Lottery

A couple of days after Kerry Yorke won the Lottery she came into my uncle's agency. She didn't bother to knock on the door that said *ANTHONY HAMER INVESTIGATIONS INC;* she just flung it open, walked in and announced herself. "I'm Kerry Yorke and I'm here to see the top man."

I was sitting at my desk, just about to bite into a tuna mayonnaise roll. I put it down when she placed a wad of twenty-pound notes in front of me. It sat about five centimetres deep. I looked up at her and blinked a few times, stupidly.

"Where's your boss? I need to see him. I can pay, too, I'm not asking for handouts. I got the money. There's plenty more where that came from."

She had a loud voice and it went perfectly with her looks. She was tall and thin as a whippet, with cheekbones you could hang pictures on. Her hair was white-blonde, the kind that had been overdyed and looked like the fringes of a carpet. Her clothes were tightly fitted: a short purple-leather skirt and jacket to match. Over the top of it was a long cream mac and on her shoulder hung a solid leather bag with a gold link strap. Her outfit looked like it had cost a lot of money.

"Won't you take a seat?" I said, picking the wad of money up and walking towards Tony's door. "I'll just see if Mr Hamer's available."

My uncle was behind his computer, his back hunched into the screen. The sound of the keys tapping away filled the room. Over the last few weeks he seemed to have been permanently in that position and often didn't answer the phone when I buzzed through; more often he didn't answer me when I spoke to him. His wife, my aunt Geraldine, had complained loudly, "Since he got that computer he doesn't communicate with anyone, he thinks of nothing else, he doesn't even bother with his own appearance any more!"

I quite liked it that way. It meant that a lot of work outside the office was left to me. It also meant that he had stopped looking in the mirror for hours on end and asking me if I thought his hair looked all right.

I placed the wad of money in front of him. After a couple of seconds he stopped typing and looked at it and then at me.

"She's in the outside office. Her name is Kerry Yorke and she wants to see you. Money's no object, apparently."

Without a word my uncle got up, brushed his clothes down and walked to my office. I could hear him speaking in his nicest voice and saw him leading her through.

"Do come in, Miss…or is it Mrs?…Yorke. Take a seat and we'll be able to discuss your case. Would you like a tea? Coffee? Some biscuits? Patricia, could you manage a couple of coffees and some biscuits? Thank you, dear."

I left them in the office and went outside to see if I could *manage* a couple of coffees.

I didn't know then that Kerry Yorke had just won the Lottery, nor that she was the mother of one of the river Lea victims.

After taking the coffee and pink wafer biscuits in, I sat down at my desk and began to speculate as to why she had come to the agency. Unfaithful husband? Missing person? Financial crime? None of them seemed to fit my image of her.

It was unusual for clients to just turn up at the office. An investigative agency wasn't like a shop where people popped in and out to see if they needed any of the services. It wasn't even that easy to find. Although we had a small sign outside it was hardly noticeable unless you were looking for it. People usually came because they were referred by someone or they had found us in the Yellow Pages and had rung up first to make an appointment.

In any case my uncle usually worked for solicitors, insurance companies or security firms. Recently, he'd taken to sub-contracting these cases out to a couple of old police force friends who worked freelance. He said he was fed up with traipsing the streets and was happier manning the computer at headquarters. He'd also given me more responsibility, allowing me to work with the insurance company people, checking out claims.

So the idea of a case walking through the door of the agency unannounced was downright odd. I wrote Kerry Yorke's name in the book beside the time and date. I'd find out why she had come soon enough.

While I was thinking of these things the intercom light went on. I clicked the switch and my uncle's voice sounded.

"Patricia, come in here a moment, Miss Yorke would like a word."

I went into my uncle's office. Kerry Yorke was sitting in the big armchair, her long legs crossed. My uncle was perched on the corner of the desk opposite her. He was smiling as if they'd both been sharing a joke. Kerry Yorke handed me a newspaper cutting. It was old, and yellowy round the edges. The headline was KID DETECTIVE FINDS MURDERER.

"That's you, isn't it?" Kerry Yorke said, a single, long finger pointing at me.

I nodded, my mouth pursed in annoyance again at the headline. It came from a local newspaper report of a case that I'd been involved in six months or so before. A reporter had interviewed me and commented on my youthfulness. He'd gone for a snappy headline and it had taken the focus off the victim and made the case seem trivial. I still hadn't forgiven him.

"About a year ago, my daughter Susie got murdered down by the river Lea. You might remember it. Another kid was killed as well. They had their hands tied up with pink ribbon. It was all over the newspapers. They called it the Gift-wrap Murders."

She smiled as she said it. It was an iron smile, solid and defensive.

"That's newspapers for you," my uncle said, with an awkward little laugh. "Anything to sell copies."

"I know. At the time I didn't mind because at least they'd stopped thinking that my Susie had drowned because of a silly game. I thought, with all the headlines they'll find the murderer. Someone will remember something and he'll be picked up, put away."

"There was a lot of police work put into it," I said. The police officer friend of mine had told me that they'd been determined to catch whoever had done it. They'd spent hours interviewing, searching for witnesses and clues. Nothing had turned up, though.

"Yes, eventually. *Eventually*. But when my Susie drowned they took one look at her and came to the conclusion that she'd brought it on herself. She was homeless, jobless, she probably hadn't even washed in a while. She'd had booze, she'd been at parties, she'd mixed with the wrong sort. Then Jennifer Ryan was found and they looked at her posh family, her home, her college books and said that it must have been murder."

"There *was* a delay starting the investigation," I said, remembering the story.

"I was angry at the time," Kerry Yorke said, "but not any more. I just wonder, when I think about it, what clues were lost in that month between the two deaths."

"By itself, Susan's death did look like an accidental drowning," I said. I wasn't defending the police but I had to be honest. Kerry Yorke didn't seem to hear me.

"Miss Yorke wants us to look for the killer of her daughter," Tony said, leaning forward with the wad of money in his hand. "I've told her that we'll help her all we can."

"I'm not sure that's such a good idea," I said.

"Patricia!" my uncle said.

"Why not?" Kerry Yorke said.

"Of course we'll take your case, Miss Yorke," my uncle said, amid coughs of indignation.

"The police investigated those murders for months," I said. "If they couldn't find anything with all their resources, how on earth could we?" I avoided looking at Tony.

"I appreciate your honesty, Patricia." Kerry Yorke gave my uncle a sideways look that seemed to silence him. "The thing is, I've never had much in my life. You know how it is, usual story. Got pregnant when I was sixteen, had Susie, and ended up living in a council flat with a string of useless boyfriends, scratching round to pay the bills, buy something nice for Susie, for me, keep some food on the table, pay for the fags and a night out. It wasn't much to ask. My Susie and me, we were close. At least, when she was little, we were. When she grew up it became harder and harder. I got together with this bloke called Benny and there was more money but it didn't work out. My Susie left one day. Just left. There was a note perched up behind the kettle. *I can't stop, Mum, I'm going away.* That's all it said. I thought, *She'll be back. She'll be back within a week.* But she didn't come back. She phoned me on Christmas Day, nine o'clock in the morning, long before Benny got up, and said she was all right, happy, living somewhere with a job."

Kerry Yorke's voice had got lower and lower and she stopped for a minute as if thinking hard.

"Next thing I knew there was a police car outside my door. They'd found a body in the river."

"It was a terrible thing," I said, "but if the police spent months on it how could we find out anything new?"

"Two Saturdays ago I won the Lottery. Six numbers. I ended up with almost a million quid. A million quid, can you believe it?"

There was nothing I could say. I glanced at my uncle and I could see his eyes, trancelike, thinking no doubt about the million pounds.

"I'm not a fool. I know you might not be able to find the murderer but I want someone new to look it all over. I've been in touch with that policewoman, Heather Warren, and she says she's happy to let you look at their files. The other reason I want you to do it is that you're a young woman, closer to my Susie's age. You might be able to talk to her friends, some of the homeless lot. You might be able to find out stuff the police couldn't."

"It might be a complete waste of time," I said.

"I want you to spend a bit of time on it. I'll pay the agency two thousand pounds. If nothing turns up I'll let it drop."

Kerry Yorke stood up. She wasn't waiting for an answer. My uncle leapt up and ran to open the door for her. He was still holding on to the wad of notes, his face a little calmer by then.

"I'm buying a house. In Woodford. Nice classy part of London. Old-fashioned, no net curtains. You know the type of place. I'll ring you when I get the phone number. Oh, and you'll be wanting this."

She unzipped her leather handbag and gave me a photograph of a teenager. A pretty girl with short dark hair and a wide smile that looked like the beginning of a giggle.

"That's my Susie," she said.

"OK," I said, "I'll have a look at the police files. But I'm not promising anything."

"That's fair enough," she said and left.

I could still smell her perfume after she'd gone. Something expensive, I thought.

17

# 3

# News

"A million pounds!" My mum let a little whistle escape her mouth. She was wrestling with a bottle of red wine, holding it between her knees and using all her strength to twist the corkscrew into the cork.

Her boyfriend of the last year or so, Gerry Lawrence, was sitting on the other side of the kitchen table, his feet up on another chair, his arms folded across his protruding belly. Behind his penny glasses I could see him blinking in a jolly way.

"A millionaire!" he said, wistfully.

"There!" Mum said, when what sounded like a loud hiccup popped out of the bottle. Gerry held his glass out immediately.

They were unpacking a take-away Indian meal.

The table was covered in small foil boxes and the air was full of the spicy aroma of the food. My stomach was making growling sounds and my mum handed me a warm plate from the oven.

"Help yourself," Gerry said, pointing his fork generously at all the dishes.

I didn't bother to say thank you because I was sure the food had been bought with my mum's money and that he was tucking into yet another free meal at her expense.

"You could live on the interest on a million pounds. You wouldn't have to work another day in your life," Gerry said, his eyes gazing into the distance.

That was rich. Gerry Lawrence had been a mature student for quite a few years and hadn't had an actual job for some time before that.

"Come on, Patsy, tuck in!" my mum said, giving me a warm smile.

I filled my plate with Indian food and went into the other room.

I put the TV on and lowered the sound. I could hear Gerry Lawrence's voice from the other room, low and husky. My mum's voice seemed to flutter above it, the odd laugh coming out, the sound of forks scraping across the plates. I ate some of my food and deliberately pushed the pair of them out of my mind and thought about Kerry Yorke and her Lottery win.

A million pounds. It was an unbelievable dream. Kerry Yorke who had been poor all her life would never have to work again. She'd move to a posh house with a big garden. She'd buy whatever furniture she wanted and a car or two. She might buy a summer house or villa, somewhere warm. She'd go on as many holidays as she liked and maybe even employ someone to do her cleaning.

Her daughter had died, though, in a horrible way, at the hands of some unbalanced person. If that wasn't bad enough, Kerry hadn't seen Susan for three months or so because she'd left home after a row about her mother's boyfriend.

I remembered being at school years before, a gang of us hanging round in the well of a staircase, hugging the radiators for warmth on a day when the wind was so sharp it felt serrated. About six of us would sit cross-legged on the floor and discuss the meaning of life – either that or what had happened on telly the night before. This particular day someone had raised the question, "If someone offered you a thousand pounds to let them cut off your finger, what would you do?"

It had made us smile, the ridiculousness of it. Billy, then my best friend, had been the least willing to discuss such an unrealistic subject.

"Who on earth would do that?" he'd said, taking it literally.

We'd all laughed, even Billy. He had known, just

like the rest of us, that that hadn't been the point. How much money was something worth to you? For a thousand pounds we could have bought most of what we wanted. How important was a little finger anyway?

"What about a kidney?" someone else had said. "If someone offered you ten thousand pounds for a kidney? Or a lung?"

"Or one hundred thousand pounds for your eyes!" someone else had said.

It was getting silly, but the conversation had gone on and on with Billy interrupting and saying that it was against the law anyway and there was no guarantee that your body part would fit anyone else's.

The bell for afternoon school had finished the discussion and we'd all uncurled, pulled ourselves away from the radiators and stumbled off to our respective lessons.

Kerry Yorke had got a million pounds and I'd have been willing to bet that she'd have returned every penny of it if she could turn back the clock and still have her daughter around.

I took my empty plate into the kitchen and put it by the sink. My mum had gone upstairs and Gerry was digging the final scraps out of the foil trays on to his plate.

"How much did you say she was paying Tony, Pats?" he said. He was the only person in the world who had ever called me by that name. Sometimes I didn't mind. That day it annoyed me.

"Two thousand pounds," I said, clicking the kettle on.

"Old Tony's rolling in it then! Make sure he gives you a big bonus."

"Tony's got a lot of expenses," I said, annoyed by his focusing on the money.

"Still, if it's you who's following the case up, shouldn't it be you who gets the lion's share?"

"It's a business," I said, tersely.

My mum came in then and ruffled Gerry's hair while I poured boiling water on to a tea bag.

"Pour me one, will you, love?" she said, and I turned to the cupboard to get another cup.

"And me, Pats." I heard Gerry's voice behind me and closed my eyes with annoyance.

I had a shower and put my dressing gown on. Then I went downstairs to watch the late news on the telly. Gerry had gone home and I could hear my mum moving about in the kitchen. I watched the screen with half an eye and started to think about Jennifer Ryan, the second girl who had been fished out of the river Lea a month after Susan Yorke's body was found. She had been a college student, in her first year of A-levels. She'd come from a "respectable" background, in a well-off neighbourhood. Yet she'd ended up just as dead as Susan. The two girls had been killed by the same person, all the available evidence pointed towards that, so there must have been something that linked them. Even though the girls hadn't known each other or, by all accounts, had never even met each other there had to be something, some factor that they had in common.

My mum came into the room and sat down on the chair beside me.

"Are you thinking about the case?" she said, softly.

"Yes," I smiled.

"I can always tell. You've got this kind of look on your face, like you're somewhere else in your head, I mean," she said, grabbing my hand with unexpected affection.

"I'm going to the police station tomorrow to pick up the files," I said.

"So you'll be quite busy, in the immediate future, I mean."

"Probably," I said. "It's really just a lot of footwork, checking over what the police have already done. I'm absolutely sure I won't find anything."

"Only I was wondering if you'd mind very much…"

"I wanted to turn the case down but you know Tony, once he saw the wad of money…" I shook my head.

"Gerry's flatmate has his mother coming over

from Australia for a couple of weeks and he asked Gerry if she could stay in his room…"

"I'll just speak to a few of the witnesses again, stuff like that. I'm sure that nothing new will turn up…"

"So Gerry will have nowhere to stay."

"What?" I said, aware that we were both talking in different directions.

"Would you mind if Gerry stayed here for a fortnight? Just while his friend's mother is visiting from Australia. He wouldn't get in your way. I'd make sure of that."

I looked at her with dismay. Gerry Lawrence staying in the house for two weeks!

"He'll have nowhere to go otherwise," my mum said, a concerned look on her face.

"Two weeks?" I said.

"That's all. You'll be working most of the time anyway. You'll hardly notice he's here. You might even get to like him!"

"I do like him!" I lied.

"That's all right, then," she said cheerfully. "He'll be moving in on Saturday and on Sunday we're going out to see some friends. We'll be out all day. Like I said, you'll hardly notice he's around."

"Right," I said, glumly.

Two weeks. How bad could it be? It was only fourteen days.

\* \* \*

The next day was Friday and I went into the local police station. My friend, Detective Inspector Heather Warren, had arranged for me to pick up photocopies of the file documents for the Susan Yorke and Jennifer Ryan murders. The desk sergeant looked at me with deep suspicion. I had to show him three different forms of identification before he handed over two giant envelopes that were packed full of stuff.

I had the weekend to read them and then I was planning to officially start following up the case on Monday.

It was going to be a busy week.

# 4

# Police Files

The police had done their work with incredible thoroughness. On Saturday I unpacked the files marked Susan Yorke and Jennifer Ryan. I then made several new piles joining the various documents together. There were photographs, statements, forensic reports, scene-of-crime reports, case up-dates and other miscellaneous stuff.

My detective friend had been as efficient as ever. In an envelope there was a note addressed to me. It read:

*Patsy, here are copies of just about everything related to these murders. I have to say that we put every possible effort into closing this case. Hundreds of hours of police work went into following all the leads. We looked at every link between these girls. I honestly don't think there's much chance of you finding anything new. I only pass the stuff on to you because I feel sorry for Kerry Yorke and think that maybe it will do her some good if she thinks it's all been looked over again.*

*All the very best,*
*Heather Warren.*
*PS Ring me if you want to talk.*

On Sunday my mum went out for the day with Gerry. I spent the whole morning reading through the different piles of information, making my own detailed notes. In the afternoon I read over it again using a highlighter pen to mark things that I thought were significant. Finally, when my eyes felt sore with concentration, I went and had a shower, packed all the stuff up to take into work the next day, got my notepad and went out to see Billy.

It was just getting dark as I walked along the backstreets to where Billy lived. The sky was clear of clouds, a flat blue, like someone's ceiling. In the distance I could see the lights of a plane twinkling and I followed its path for a few moments. I wondered where it was going: USA? Spain? Turkey? It might be interesting, I thought idly, to be strapped into the seat of a plane on my way somewhere exotic. I gave a light sigh and went on my way, walking briskly towards the neighbourhood where Billy lived.

I couldn't help but think about the case.

Susan Yorke had always been an odd, withdrawn kid. She'd lived with her mum in a council flat all her life, gone to the local school, had a couple of friends for short periods. Mostly she had been a real loner. The person she seemed to have got on best with was her mother, Kerry. She and Kerry spent most of their time together. Then her mother found a boyfriend, Benny Gold, a market trader who was several years older than Kerry. They were together for about a year, and even though Benny had his own flat, he often stayed with Kerry and Susan for weeks at a time. There'd never been any talk of marriage.

Susan hadn't liked him at all, apparently, and there'd been nasty rows. Eventually Susan left home and shortly after that the relationship between her mother and Benny Gold had ended. It was too late for Susan, though. There was evidence that Kerry had looked for her daughter relentlessly but had no luck in finding her.

There was some bitty information that pin-pointed Susan's whereabouts in the months after she left home. A number of homeless people had come forward and said that they remembered her living on the streets around Whitechapel and she occasionally used a hostel called St Michael's. She was documented as having used the Crisis centre over the Christmas period where she had a roof over her head, medical and dental treatment and access to a phone. This was when she'd rung her mother.

In January, she'd used St Michael's hostel occasionally and a couple of charity kitchens for food. Mostly, though, it seems she'd hung around with a crowd of young kids who'd liked to get drunk and party. The next thing anyone knew was that she was found with her lungs full of water in the river Lea.

I got to Billy's street a few minutes later and quickened my pace towards his front door. I hadn't seen him for a couple of days and I was looking forward to telling him about the case. He answered his front door in a dressing gown, his mouth foaming with toothpaste.

"Am I early?" I said, walking past him.

He nodded and made a ten sign with his fingers.

"Ten minutes," I said. "I'll wait in the kitchen."

I heard his feet padding back up the stairs as I went into the small kitchen and picked up the kettle. I stood waiting for it to boil and looked around the room and smiled.

A couple of weeks before, Billy and I had decorated it. We'd gone to a local trading estate and bought paint, wallpaper, tiles and new floor covering. We'd spent days preparing the room by peeling the old wallpaper off, sandpapering the paintwork, digging the old cracked tiles off the wall. We'd emptied the cupboards and bought some new doors for the units.

It had been a lot of work but it had been worth it. Not just because the room was light and clean and attractive to look at, but because it had been the first time Billy had done anything to the house since his parents had been killed in a car crash almost four years before.

It was the house he had grown up in. When I had first known him at secondary school he had invited me back there to see his new computer, to watch videos, to have pizzas or take-away curries. His mum and dad, very prim and proper people, had liked me even though they'd found me loud and weren't keen on the clothes I wore.

When they'd been killed Billy had taken it in a very adult way. At least that was what people had said. But then he had always been "grown up"; right from the age of eleven he'd had the sound of a sensible forty-five-year-old about him. Of course he handled his parents' deaths sensibly. It was what everyone expected of him.

In the weeks and months afterwards it had been a different story. He had dropped out of school, stopped caring about himself. He told me he'd felt like he was at the bottom of a deep black hole and could see no way to pull himself out of it. I'd gone round on my way home from school and gossiped and chatted. A lot of times he hadn't wanted to see me but I'd persevered, pestered him, nagged him, *forced* him to come back into the world again.

I made myself a cup of tea and sat down at the table where there were a number of leaflets strewn about. That was a surprise. Billy's kitchen table was usually covered in bits of car engines. I picked one up and saw the headline, *A YEAR OF YOUR LIFE TO HELP OTHERS*. Another said *AFRICA AID: Young people who give up a year to give a life to desperate communities.*

*Junk mail*, I thought and swept them aside so that I could look at my notebook. I turned to the pages on Jennifer Ryan and read through while I was sipping my tea.

Jennifer Ryan had lived with her mum and dad. Jenny, as she was called, had excelled at school and had been very popular. She'd been at a sixth-form college in east London and had been studying A-level English, media studies and sociology. She lived a normal teenage life, working at college and going out with friends. She'd recently broken up with a boyfriend and there was a suggestion that she might have been seeing someone new on the quiet. In the weeks before she was murdered she'd been having some dental treatment. On the night of March 14th she'd gone out to meet someone at the Willow Tree pub on the river Lea. No one had turned up, though, and she'd waited for a while, had rather too many drinks and walked off into the night.

That was the last time anyone saw her alive.

"Hi." Billy's voice broke into my thoughts.

"Oh, I didn't hear you come down the stairs," I said, closing up my notepad.

"Where are we going?" he said.

I looked at him for a moment. His face looked flushed from the shower and his hair was still wet. I could smell soap and shampoo and aftershave. He was wearing a shirt that I'd bought him for Christmas and jeans that were years old, faded with time. I felt a glow of something in my chest.

"Cinema? A drink? I don't really mind," I said, putting away my notepad.

"Found any links? Between the two girls, I mean?" he said, scooping up the leaflets that had been scattered about the table.

"Just two," I said, picking my jacket up. "At least, I didn't find them, they were investigated by the police at the time. Apparently, both girls had used the same dentist. Susan, the homeless girl, had some treatment in the Crisis shelter at Christmas. Jennifer had some treatment in February and March."

"But the police have looked into it?" he said.

"Yes. It was an obvious lead. The other interesting link is that Susan occasionally used a hostel called St Michael's, down by the docks, and Jennifer Ryan was involved in community service at her college. The students from there sometimes work on a voluntary basis at St Michael's. There's no evidence that the girls ever met, though."

"If the police looked into it and didn't find anything, why reopen the case?" Billy was putting his coat on and looking for his car keys.

"Kerry Yorke, Susan's mother, wants it looked into again. She's hoping that something was missed and she thinks that because I'm younger I might have more luck in getting information."

"Is that likely? The case had a lot of publicity at the time."

"I know, I know," I said, mildly irked, "I've said all that. I've told her honestly that I don't think I'll find anything but…"

"She's paying the agency a lot of money," he said, and looked at me with jokey disapproval. I felt my previous good mood dissipating.

"I did try to refuse the case!" I said, following Billy out to the car.

He didn't answer, just gave me a sardonic smile. I got into the passenger seat disgruntled and found another couple of leaflets like those that had been on the kitchen table. *TAKE A YEAR OUT: CHARITY WORK IN CENTRAL AMERICA.*

*More junk mail*, I thought, and folded my arms grumpily.

# 5

# Scene-of-Crime

I decided to approach the case in a methodical way. I was going to focus on the links. I was going to visit and talk to the people at the hostel and also see the dentist. I wasn't going to close my eyes to other possible links, either.

The police had done their job well, I knew that. I really didn't expect to find anything. That's what I told myself even though I knew it was a lie. Deep inside I had this ardent desire to find something that they had missed.

Don't get me wrong, I'm not in competition with the police or anything like that. It's just that in the past there's been times that they've been so certain they were right that they've told me off, forbidden me to pursue a lead or made me feel downright foolish.

This time I had no theory. I was starting with a completely open mind and a huge amount of information that I hoped would lead me somewhere new, somewhere beyond the police investigation.

I had arranged to go and see Kerry Yorke the next day. That afternoon I was heading for the river Lea, to where it all started.

After breakfast I went up to my room to get ready. I grabbed a long skirt and a jumper and pulled my blue DMs out from under the bed. I washed my face and applied some moisturizer. I stood for a moment wondering whether to put some make-up on. A dab of lipstick was all I felt like. I reached up to the top of my wardrobe and pulled down a velour hat that I'd been given for Christmas. It was light grey and fitted snugly over my head with the brim pulled floppily down on my forehead.

I loved that hat. My mum had bought it for me from some catalogue and it could be folded up in the bottom of a bag or in a deep pocket for days and still spring back to its original shape.

I've got this whole collection of hats that I've saved over the years. They sit on top of my wardrobe in various carrier bags and hat boxes that my mum has picked up for me. I'd taken to wearing the same one for ages and then when I was thoroughly fed up with it, I'd pull them all down and choose another. I'd been wearing the velour hat for weeks but I still liked the way it changed my appearance. I don't say that it made me look better, but it did make me look *different*.

I emptied my rucksack on to the bed and threw away several sweet wrappers and scrunched up tissues. Into it I put a small automatic camera that my uncle had loaned me. I also picked up a handful of cards with the words *Patsy Kelly, Investigative Work, Good Rates* printed on them. Underneath was the office address and phone number and the number of my mobile. My plan was to go to the area where the girls had been found, take some photographs and talk to people.

I went downstairs just as my mum was packing her briefcase ready to go to work. She was wearing a tweed suit and red blouse. She had black court shoes on and a black shoulder bag. Her hair was up at the back in a tight pleat that she had taken to wearing. She looked round at me and her face dropped.

"Patsy! You're not going out in those boots and that hat! I'm beginning to wish I'd never bought it for you. When are you going to start dressing nicely?"

I was just about to answer when Gerry came walking out of the kitchen. He was wearing a wrinkled shirt that his stomach was poking through with old track-suit bottoms. His hair was standing up in the middle and his socks had holes in them.

My mum looked at him and then at me and walked off up the hall, a great sigh coming from her.

"I give up," she said. "I really do give up."

Gerry and I smiled at each other, for once on the same side of an argument.

The river Lea stretches from the centre of London northwards towards Hertfordshire. The area that I was interested in was where it ran through Hackney in between several closed-down factories. The entry to the river was through a small group of houses and shops and a pub.

I got a bus there and cursed myself for the hundredth time for not getting on with the business of passing my driving test. The trouble was that even though I'd been learning to drive for about eighteen months, I had simply never needed to put in for my test. I always had my mum or my uncle or Billy to drive with me. More often, though, I let Billy drive me about in one of the cars he was working on.

The previous night I'd asked him if he could take me down to Hackney but he said he'd be "busy". I wondered if he'd gone back to looking for a job. I'd known for a while that he'd been fed up with doing up old cars and selling them on. It wasn't as if he needed the money, his parents' death had left him quite comfortable, but I could tell that he was getting bored and needed something proper to do.

It meant that I was definitely going to have to take my driving test.

The bus dropped me off outside a small row of

shops and I took the alley between them that led me down to the river. Facing on to the water was the garden of the Willow Tree, all the seats up-ended. A few metres along was a small fast-food stall, a trailer that had been towed there and parked up at the side of the river. It was called *Aquarius Foods*. There was no one around so I took a couple of photos and walked on.

There was a plaque at the river's edge which read *JUBILEE WALKWAY. Please take your litter with you.* Underfoot it was muddy and I had to step carefully. I passed by a number of Victorian brick buildings, huge chimneys sticking up into the sky, strangely quiet. At the side, facing on to the river, was a loading bay, gaping like an open mouth. I clicked the camera three or four times, feeling more like a student compiling a portfolio than a detective.

I walked further on to where a main road crossed the river via a concrete bridge. Underneath, the daylight was squeezed out as the walkway itself became wider. I could see clearly but it was grey and dingy and I had to be careful to sidestep the thick columns that were dotted about like looming tree trunks. The traffic noises were muted and there was a heavy hush amid which I could hear the clinking of the steel caps on my boots. The surfaces were all covered in garish graffiti; the signatures of the young kids who hung around the area, like cave paintings of a modern era. Using the flash I took more pictures and then quickened my steps to get out from under the oppressive atmosphere.

A couple of barges were parked just beyond the bridge. A tall, thin man was cleaning the windows of one of them with a chamois. Every few seconds he stepped back, looked at the glass and then continued polishing.

"Good morning," I said.

He turned towards me, his forehead creased up. He was wearing a thick army-type jumper over corduroy trousers. On his hands were a pair of dark green rubber gloves.

"Spring cleaning?" I said, pointing at the windows.

"Yes," he said, stopping what he was doing. "I thought I'd make a start while it's dry."

"I was wondering if you could help me," I said, getting to the point. "I'm looking into the deaths of Susan Yorke and Jennifer Ryan. You'll probably remember, it all happened just over a year ago."

"Oh, terrible," he said, squeezing the chamois tightly until a couple of drops of water came out. "Didn't they ever get anyone for that?"

"No, Mr…?"

"Dawkins, Roger Dawkins."

"Patsy Kelly," I said and held my hand out for him to shake. "Have you been moored here a long time?" His name rang a distant bell in my head; probably from one of the witness statements I'd read over the weekend.

"A year last Christmas. Retired from the army ten years ago. Wife died year before last. Been out and about on the boat ever since."

"It's very smart," I said, looking at its bold green-and-red paintwork and its glittering windows.

"Regular maintenance, cleaning and she's good as new."

"Doesn't it ever move?"

"Only if the rent gets too steep."

"You were here then, when the girls were killed."

"I was. The police interviewed me. I told them I saw the first girl round this area for a couple of days with a gang of scruffs, you know, that homeless lot. They were creating a nuisance, to tell you the truth, sitting on the river bank with their cans of lager. Freezing cold, it was."

"You definitely remembered Susan Yorke."

"Definitely. She was a cheeky madam. I had a to-do with her one day when I saw her getting out of this van in the pub car park. I thought I'd have a quiet word with her, about the eyesore her and her pals were creating along the river. She told me to shove off and mind my own business. Bloke in the van sent a great spray of water at me, covered I was, head to foot."

I remembered his witness statement then. The van had belonged to a company of some sort. He hadn't been able to remember what it was called only that it was to do with plants or farming.

Neither had he been able to remember the colour, only that it was a dark van. He'd only glanced at it, he'd said, he'd been much more involved in the argument with the girl. The police had looked for the van, they'd even used it as part of the *CRIME-FILE* spot on TV but no one had ever come forward.

"Do you mind if I take a few photos?" I said. "I'm just trying to get a feel of the area."

"Certainly, I'm always proud to have my boat in pictures," he said and smiled widely.

After I'd taken the shot, I gave Mr Dawkins one of my cards to keep in case he remembered anything new and then I walked on.

The place where Susan's body was found was just a couple of hundred metres on. The buildings seemed to disappear and for a stretch of about twenty metres or so all I could see was green grass and bushes. I walked towards a bench that had a small plaque with *Waterside* written on it. I sat down and looked straight ahead, across the river to where the huts of a rowing club were grouped. A couple of people in sporty clothes were milling around. To the left was the gentle bend of the river where Jennifer Ryan had been found, large clumps of reeds standing like pampas grass against the sky. To the right I could see the barges and the concrete bridge that I had just passed under. I picked up the camera and took photos of all of them from where I was sitting. Behind me was an area of rough ground with shrubs and trees, and beyond that, what looked like a road leading through some disused allotments.

After I'd finished taking pictures I walked back towards the Willow Tree. I waved to Mr Dawkins on his barge and went back under the concrete bridge. The pub garden was still empty but *Aquarius Foods* was opening up. A short young man of about twenty was taking shutters off the side of the trailer and I could see the bars of an electric fire inside.

"Hi," I said, rubbing my hands together. "Any chance of a cup of tea?"

"Five minutes," he said, without looking at me.

"I'll wait," I said. Out of the corner of my eye, I saw an older man walking along with two carrier bags, one in each hand. He got to the van and put each of the bags on to the counter. I smiled cheerfully at him.

"You're an early bird," he said, looking at his watch.

"Yes," I said brightly, looking at each of them in turn.

They were related, it was obvious. The older man was just a touch taller than me, with a hard, round stomach and generous double chin. He had thick dark hair that was streaked with grey. The younger man's hair was raven black, cropped into his head except for a single pigtail plait that hung down his thick, red neck. He looked solid, but rounded.

"Can we get you anything?" the older man said. "Or are you just passing by?" He began to unload bread rolls from one of the carrier bags.

"Just some tea, please. I'm actually here looking into a couple of murders that happened along the river about a year ago," I said.

"The two girls?" the older man said. "We heard about it, didn't we, Ian? Dreadful, dreadful."

"You weren't here when it happened?"

"No. We only opened up last June."

"Eighteenth of June to be precise," the younger one said, handing me a cup of tea. I noticed that behind him on the wall of the trailer were several posters: female pop bands, soap stars, horoscopes, boxers and footballers.

"Was there someone here before you? Another café?"

"No, I don't believe there was. Not much call for it. River fell out of fashion, you see. Last couple of years have been better, though. These new walkways have opened the river up again and you get a lot more people down here. No, me and Ian, my son that is, we saw an advertisement for this pitch, last Easter I think, and we thought we could make a go of it."

"Right," I said, not really too interested in the history of the river Lea.

"You're a policewoman, are you?" the older man said.

"No, I'm a private detective. We're looking into the case again, just a kind of final check to make sure that nothing was missed."

I got out a card and handed it to him.

"Oh," he said, looking closely at it. "Private detective! Well. I thought they only had those things in the United States of America." There was a smile around the corners of his lips and I felt miffed for a minute, thinking that he was making fun of me.

"Patsy Kelly, well I never. I'm Alan Payne, this here's my son, Ian. If you like, I'll keep this card and I'll mention it to some of the regulars. You never know who might remember something."

"Would you? Thanks ever so much." I turned away, imagining him raising eyebrows with several other old river-fogies, saying "well I never" and pointing at my card which would probably end up pinned on the wall beside the horoscopes and soap stars.

"Here, I'll pay you for this," I said, pointing to my tea.

"No," Alan Payne said. "On the house."

"Thanks a lot," I said, grateful for the generous gesture, and walked off towards the pub.

The landlord of the Willow Tree was one of the rudest men I have ever spoken to. His name was Robert Pettifer Wilson and he had longish grey hair, a paisley bowtie and a checked waistcoat. He spoke loudly and without the benefit of full stops.

"I've got a delivery coming in fifteen minutes and I've been all through this damned business over and over I lost money in those weeks when it all happened with the police running back and forth searching for this and that and not allowing the public around here in case they walked off with any important clues I'm damned if I'm wasting any of my time going over the whole thing again."

I didn't bother to try and butt in. I just got out my card and offered it in a little girl's voice, only to have it snatched from me and stuck on a noticeboard behind the till.

"Don't bother to show me out," I said under my breath, as I walked through the saloon bar and back into the alley that led to the street.

Back in the office I ate a sandwich with a freshly made cup of tea and opened up a new file on the computer. I spent the rest of the day putting the information from the files into different documents under my own new headings: *Scene-of-Crime, Local Witness Statements, Forensic, Victim Similarities, Victim Differences* and so on.

By the time four o'clock had come, my eyes were popping out of my head with tiredness. I had started to pack up, when my uncle Tony came in carrying a big cardboard box.

"Patricia, give me a hand with this, will you?" He was grunting with exertion.

We unpacked a small photocopier. It sat on the desk looking creamy and elegant and most of all *new*.

"Where'd you get this?"

"Bought it. Got a good discount for cash. Plus I paid some outstanding accounts at British Telecom. The bank manager's looking a lot happier as well."

He went off into his office and I looked at the photocopier with a creeping feeling of dismay. He had already spent a lot of Kerry Yorke's money and I hadn't even started the case properly. I could hear him humming gaily in the other room.

"I'm going home," I shouted, gathering my stuff together.

"See you," he answered. I could hear furniture being moved around, most probably he was looking for a place to put the photocopier. I went out the office door and let it close with a bang behind me.

He hadn't even asked me about the case. All he cared about was the money.

# 6

# Kerry Yorke

"I'll drop you off in Woodford, Patsy, but I can't hang around. I've got some things to do today."

Billy pulled out into the traffic on the dual carriageway and I felt our speed increase.

"Are you in a rush?" I said, miffed because I had hoped that he'd be able to come with me to see Kerry Yorke.

"Not exactly, but I've got somewhere to go."

"Oh," I said. "Are you going to see a car?"

"No," he said. "I saw some interesting stuff in the papers the other day about a job. I'm just going to check some stuff out. I won't say anything yet, in case nothing materializes."

I'd been right then. Billy was still looking for a job.

He'd started talking about a career a while before, after he'd sold a red Ford Capri that he'd been working on. We'd met the buyer in a pub, a young man of about twenty-five in an expensive designer jacket who'd taken one brief look at the car and agreed the price straight away. He'd given Billy an envelope full of fifty-pound notes. Billy had given the man the keys and sat drinking quietly, the envelope of money sitting on the table between us.

"Put it away," I'd said, looking round the pub, sure that we were being watched from each corner.

He'd shoved the envelope in his pocket. After a few seconds he spoke. "I worked on that car for three weeks solidly. I did every bit of it myself. Now it's gone. He hardly looked at it for more than sixty seconds."

"That's because he knew it was good," I said.

"No, he just wanted a Capri. He didn't care that I'd spent all my time matching up the interior fabric or finding the right-shaped headlight sockets."

"But he paid you the price you wanted."

"That's not the point. You know I don't do it for the money."

"What is the point then?"

"I don't know. That's the point. I just don't know," he'd said, irritated.

We'd left our drinks unfinished on the table and walked the couple of miles home along the streets of east London.

"I need to *do* something," Billy had said, after a while.

"Like?"

"A job. A place where I go to work every day. See people, have some role. Something important to do, not just messing around on old cars."

"I'd hardly call what you do just messing around on old cars!"

"I need to do something useful. Where I'd make a difference, helping people."

"You'd hate it," I'd immediately said. "You'd hate having to take orders and working with people in charge of you. Look at my uncle Tony. You'd hate having to work for someone like him."

"I don't just mean a *job* job. I know I could go and work for Big Ron down at the paint shop anyday. It's not that. I don't need the money, I just want to do something…"

"What, though?"

"I don't know. Something different."

We'd left it at that. A few days later Billy had started buying all the serious newspapers and circling job adverts. He'd started ringing round and had even written a number of letters. He'd become quickly discouraged.

"They all want someone with qualifications or experience," he'd said, bitterly.

He'd looked hard for a couple of weeks and I asked him about it from time to time but he got impatient and moody so I'd dropped the subject. I thought he'd probably figure out in time that he'd need to go to university and get a degree. That would be good for him, I was sure. It wouldn't be so bad for us either, him studying, me doing detective work. In my head I'd had it all nicely worked out.

He pulled into the side of the road in Woodford High Street and I gave him a quick kiss and got out. As he drove away I thought about him going to university, a nearby one, where he could live at home and still see me.

I found myself humming as I looked for the road that Kerry Yorke's new house was in. I found it a few minutes later and paused for a second before I opened the gate and walked in. It wasn't what I had expected. It was small for a start, quite old with ivy growing completely up one side. The windows were long and narrow and had no net curtains on them. Across the front was iron trellis-work, like sturdy lace, preventing anyone from getting in. Through them I could see a bare interior, as though the house was empty.

Just then the front door opened and she was standing there, in jeans and a huge jumper, her white-blonde hair pulled back with a black velvet band.

"Hi, Patsy!" she said cheerfully. "You found it all right?"

She had no make-up on and her face looked

scrubbed. She looked much younger than the first time we had met, not much more than a kid herself.

"Come in. I want to show you something funny," she said and I followed her into the hallway, her feet in high-heeled boots clattering ahead of me, echoing in the empty hallway.

"It's a nice house," I said, even though I hadn't seen it all.

"Yes, it will be. This way."

We passed a couple of empty rooms and went down some stairs into a long kitchen. The room was warmer than the rest and I saw a huge leather chair in one corner and a table with a small colour TV opposite it. At the far corner were half a dozen wooden boxes.

"That's my worldly goods, Patsy. Would you believe it, everything I own in six boxes."

"Where's the rest?" I said. "Your furniture? Your clothes?"

"I chucked it all," she said, looking delighted with herself. "All in the bin. Without a second thought. What's there is mostly my Susie's stuff."

"Oh."

"Here, I'll put the kettle on. I've managed to buy a few things. A lot of my new stuff won't be here until later this week. Amazing, isn't it? If you've got money, you can go and buy a house in a couple of days but you can't get them to deliver a fridge or a washing machine until they're good and ready." She was shaking her head.

"It's a lovely kitchen," I said and I meant it. It was a long room with the units all down one end and a space for a table and chairs down the other. There were French doors at the end that looked out on to a small walled garden. From where I was standing I could see an ornate bird bath and behind it a garden pond. There was also a paved area and rock garden and single gold daffodils were dotted across the lawn like stars.

"I know what you're thinking," Kerry Yorke said, as she poured water into a teapot. "You're thinking it's small. For a millionaire, it's a small house." She gave a loud laugh, more like an exclamation.

"No..." I lied.

"It's small but expensive, know what I mean? It's old and it's got trees and shrubs that have been growing here for a hundred years or more. Now, I could have bought myself a really big new house but it wouldn't have had a past, a history."

"I know what you mean," I said, taking a china cup and saucer from her.

"You sit on the Chesterfield," she said, pointing to the leather chair, "I'll sit on the cushion."

She sat cross-legged on the floor and I found myself looking down on her for once. Her blonde hair was tightly pulled back from her head and I couldn't see any trace of darker roots.

"Come on, Patsy, get all your notes and files out. Let's talk about my Susie. I want you to tell me everything. It's not like I don't have all the time in the world, now is it?" She gave me an encouraging smile and I placed my cup and saucer on top of the tiny TV and dipped into my rucksack.

I liked her. For a millionaire, she was all right.

After I'd shown her all the notes I'd made and relevant details from the files, I asked her to tell me about the period that had led up to Susan leaving home, in particular about the rows between Susan and her boyfriend, Benny.

"Benny Gold. I met him down Walthamstow market. He had this jumper stall. All the famous labels, seconds. Nothing wrong with them, at least nothing you could see. I used to pass by, regularly, getting my shopping, looking at the stalls. He was older than me, a good bit older. But I'd had my fill of young blokes. They're nothing but trouble. They move in and live off you, then they start scouting round for someone else. No, I was ready for someone more solid, someone like Benny."

"He never actually lived with you?"

"Not officially, no. Towards the end, before my Susie left, he was staying most of the time. Not that he didn't pay his way, mind you. He was generous with money. Bought my Susie anything she wanted, bought food, gifts, meals out. He was a decent bloke and though I won't say I was in love with him, I was fond of him."

"But he and Susan didn't get on."

"At first they did. She seemed to like him. Then she started to get a bit funny. But that was normal for Susie. She hated anyone to get close to me. Usually though, when she saw that she was still my number one, she settled down. She knew full well that my blokes were temporary. She was the one permanent thing in my life."

Kerry Yorke stopped speaking for a moment, her lips pursed closely together.

"Did they have rows?" I said, gently prompting her.

"It all came from Susie. She started to be rude to him, to make fun of his age, his looks, his hair, his job. Whatever he said to her, she just sniped back at him. I told her off a few times, it was embarrassing. I began to feel quite sorry for Benny."

"How did she come to leave?"

"I got home one day to this terrible row. Susie and Benny shouting at each other. Susie crying and locking herself in her room. That was the worst, really. I'd never known a time when I couldn't get round her. Never."

"That's when she left."

Kerry Yorke nodded silently.

"You went to the police?"

"Course I did. They put her on the Missing Persons list. A lot of good that did."

"And when she rang you at Christmas, what did she say?"

" 'I'm all right, Mum, I've got this flat and a job. I'll call you soon.' I know the words off by heart. That was the last time I ever heard her voice."

Kerry Yorke stood up and walked across to the kitchen unit, pulled off some kitchen roll and blew her nose.

"I've cried buckets over my Susie. But they say it's all right to cry. Don't ever hold it in, that's what the counsellor said."

"What happened to Benny Gold?"

"I got rid of him. A couple of weeks after Susie left I told him to pack his bag and stuff his jumpers." She was smiling again. "I'll tell you, Patsy, I ended up with more jumpers than a normal woman could ever wear."

I found myself smiling at her, imagining piles and piles of jumpers. Her smile faded though, and she carried on talking.

"My Susie was a funny kid. She had these fads, you know, she'd be besotted with something for months on end and then suddenly change on to something else. It was some pop group for a while, then it was supporting the local football team, then it was the horoscopes. She had books about it, posters. It's all junk, I know, but I've kept the lot. All packed up. I know she'll never come back but still I've kept the lot."

There was a tremor around her mouth and I started talking to cover up her sadness.

"Here's my plan," I said. "I'm going to go to St Michael's hostel and then to the dentist's. Those were the main links that the police found. I'll see if I can jog anyone's memory."

"They know me at St Michael's. Tell them I've sent you. They're really nice."

"I'll keep you in touch, let you know if I find anything. I'll also do a day-by-day report of my activities."

"Just do what you can. I'm not expecting miracles."

"What are you going to do now?" I said, imagining her sitting day after day in a strange house in an area where she knew nobody.

"I got a few ideas," she said, touching the end of her nose with her finger.

I got up to go.

"Truth is, I can't really get straight and get started on anything new until I know that I've done everything I can to find out who killed my Susie. That's why I'm depending on you, Patsy."

Then she did an odd thing. She put one of her arms round my shoulder and hugged me. Only for a microsecond. Then she let go and walked ahead of me up the hall. I looked at her high heels, scraping along the wood floor, her long drainpipe legs, her scraggy hair, pulled into a tiny ponytail at the back.

I felt a surge of affection for her. At that moment she seemed terribly fragile, as if a strong gust of wind could blow her away.

"Keep in touch, Patsy," she said, letting me out.

I promised her I would and walked away feeling full of importance. Don't ask me why.

# 7

# A Place to Stay

St Michael's was in Whitechapel, quite close to the City. I got the tube there just after lunch. It was a couple of old Victorian houses that joined on to the side of a tiny church and a church hall. I found the man who ran it, Peter Lee, outside in the street unloading some supplies from the back of a van. I told him who I was and mentioned Kerry Yorke's name. He nodded in a businesslike way and handed me a giant bag of toilet rolls. As we walked in I noticed the heavy iron door and the wire mesh across all the windows. Peter Lee punched a number into a security lock outside and we waited to be buzzed in.

"We've had three burglaries in the last two months," he said, pushing the door in with his foot, "and our clients like to feel secure once they're inside the hostel."

He was about twenty-five and wasn't unpleasant to look at. He had short fair hair and pale skin with the shadow of stubble on his chin. He either hadn't had a chance to shave or he was cultivating a look. I must have inadvertently raised my eyebrows at his use of the word "clients". He noticed and immediately spoke to me in a clipped voice.

"What would you prefer we call them, Miss Kelly? Vagrants? Dossers? Down-and-outs?"

"I didn't mean..." I said, cross with myself for being insensitive. I followed him through two security doors and along a dark corridor to an empty common room where he dumped his supplies on the floor.

"I'm really sorry. It's just that I..." I started to say.

"It's OK, Miss Kelly. The general public's view of homeless people is that they're somewhat less than human, that they don't need to be treated with respect."

"Cool down, Peter," a loud voice came from behind me, "you've got it all wrong. If that's the same Miss Kelly I met a while ago, she's not what you think."

I turned round gratefully and was faced with a tall woman of about forty with greying hair and a mass of jewellery. She gave me a smile.

"Hello, Alice," I said relieved to see someone I knew. My eye settled on the nose-ring she was wearing. That was new. She hadn't had it the last time we'd met.

"Patsy Kelly, the kid detective. I read a piece about you in the newspaper. Still solving crime?"

"Sort of," I said, feeling myself getting embarrassed in front of Peter Lee. I handed him the toilet rolls and watched while Big Alice put her arm around him and led him out of the room.

Alice hadn't changed much. I'd first met her about eighteen months before, when I'd been involved in the murder of a girl whose body had been found in a house used by homeless people down by the river. She'd been a real help then, not just to me but to a number of young homeless kids who had ended up sleeping on the streets, with nowhere to go, no money and no hope. I'd liked her then and I was mightily pleased to see her there in the hostel where I was hoping to get some information.

"Don't be upset by Peter. He's got a difficult job and he does his best. As well as that, he's just had some personal family problems. You know what I mean, messy divorce, that kind of stuff."

"Oh," I said.

"He's quite nice, really, when you get to know him."

"Where are the people who use the hostel?" I said, not quite able to use the word "clients".

"We cater for the under-twenties but they only spend the night here. At eight in the morning they have to check out. It's only an overnight facility."

"What happens to them during the day?"

"On the streets. Some of them go to day centres, soup kitchens, church halls, places like that. A lot of them sit in shop doorways, avoiding the police; some of them beg."

I pursed my lips and thought of my own bedroom with my twenty-tog duvet, my radiators, a hot shower whenever I wanted it.

"What brings you here?" Alice said, walking into a small kitchen area. She bent down to a cupboard and pulled out a giant pot which she placed on top of what looked like an antique gas oven.

"I'm working for a woman called Kerry Yorke. You might remember that her daughter Susan was one of the two girls who were murdered down by the river Lea last year."

"I do remember it. Something about *gift-wrapping...*"

"That's right. Her mum wants me to go over the case, see if anything was overlooked. I'm sure I won't find anything but it'll probably make her feel better. Did you know her? Do you think Peter Lee will talk to me about her?"

Alice had placed four catering-sized tins of vegetable soup on the worktop and was exerting a lot of energy with a tiny tin opener. She stopped for

61

a moment, got another tin opener out of the drawer and handed it to me.

"Help me get this soup into the pot and then I'll get Peter. I've only been working in this hostel for about six months so I never had any contact with her."

I took the tin opener and watched the muscles in Alice's arms tighten as she wrestled with the lid. Then I mustered up all the strength I had and started to open another tin.

When the soup was on, Alice went into the back office and came out with Peter Lee behind her. He seemed a little more relaxed. I got out the photo I had of Susan Yorke and gave it to him.

"I remember Susan quite well," he said, when Alice had placed a mug of tea in his hand. "She was a sparky kid, you know, full of chat. She came here a few times in the autumn. We didn't see her over Christmas, but then in the January, she came from time to time."

"Why did she move on, if she had a place to stay here?" I said.

"It doesn't work that way, Miss Kelly. She didn't actually have a place to stay here." I could see Peter Lee was getting irritated again. For a young man in a responsible job he had a short fuse.

"Thing is," Alice butted in, "the hostel doesn't function like that. A place like this is only ever a last stage for these kids. We have two dormitories with about a dozen beds in each. One for males and one for females. Plus a couple of small cubicles we keep for kids with pets. It's all on a first-come-first-served basis. A lot of kids don't like that but it's all we can offer. There are hostels where kids have their own rooms but there aren't enough places to go round."

"Who staffs the place?" I said. "Apart from you?"

"We have a couple of night workers. They're fairly recent, though, and they're helped by various charity workers. We have links with the local sixth-form college and some students help out."

"The other girl who was murdered, Jennifer Ryan, she was a student at that college."

"The police asked me about her but I don't think she was part of the group that visited here. I personally don't remember her." Peter Lee left the photo on the table and went to the sink with his empty teacup. I realized then that I hadn't yet drunk any of mine.

"I thought the police had looked into all this," Peter Lee said, holding his cup under the running water.

"They did, pretty thoroughly, I think. I'm just going over stuff. Here's my card," I said, handing it to him. "If you should think of anything else my mobile phone number's on there."

Peter Lee put his washed teacup down and took my card. He looked at it without expression, then put it into a drawer.

"I need to get on, Miss Kelly. Alice, I'm doing some ringing round for funds," he said and walked off.

The kitchen door half closed behind him and I sat, feeling dissatisfied. The interview hadn't produced much. I became aware of the faint aroma of the soup heating through.

"He's not a great communicator, but he's a good bloke. I'm sure if he thinks of anything he'll get in touch," Alice said softly, putting her cup into the sink.

"I was hoping to come back this evening and talk to some of the homeless kids who use this place. I'm sort of counting on the fact that one or two of them might remember Susan Yorke."

Alice shook her head from side to side. "It's not that likely that the same kids will be staying here. They tend to move around. Anyway, I'm not sure they would talk to you. They're not good with strangers and any hint of the police or the law and they tend to clam up. You should know that from past experience."

I nodded my head. She was referring to the case we'd both been involved in. If it hadn't been for her I'd never have got the information I needed.

"Why don't you let me try?" she said. "They all know me, I could ask around, see if anyone remembers her."

"Would you?" I said, getting another card out. "I'd be really grateful."

"Why not?" she said. "It's for a good cause, after all."

A buzzer sounded, making me jump. Alice walked across to a wall phone and picked it up. After saying something she replaced the receiver and turned back.

"It's Polly, one of the night workers."

"I have to go anyway," I said, looking at my watch.

"I'll do my best and I'll get in touch if anything looks promising," Alice said, letting a small black woman in the front door as I went out. "We must meet even so, maybe have a tea somewhere?" she said, and I noticed she had a pair of earrings in the shape of question marks.

"Absolutely," I said, genuinely pleased to have seen her.

The door slammed shut behind me and I walked briskly towards the tube. Turning a corner quickly I almost tripped over a young man sitting in a sleeping bag, his legs stretched out across the pavement. His skin was waxy and dirty-looking and his eyes looked as though they'd sunk into his forehead. Curled up beside him was a brown dog, its fur chunky, its brown eyes looking up at me with more life than its owner's.

"Can you spare a few pence?" his voice came out. In his fingers was a cigarette, the ash balancing on the end.

I looked back at him, feeling sympathy mixed in

with a mild disgust. I put my hand in my pocket and gave him my spare change. It wouldn't change his life but it would make me feel better when I was curling up under my duvet.

I got home from work about six and found Gerry and my mum in the kitchen, chopping and mixing the ingredients of some dish that they were going to cook. I went up to my room and made a note of the information I had got that day. It wasn't much but I was pleased that I'd made a start and delighted that I'd made contact with Big Alice.

After a few minutes my mum came in, holding her sticky hands out in front of her.

"Patsy, I forgot to say. Billy called a while ago. He says he's got some good news but he can't see you until tomorrow night when he'll tell you about it."

"Did he say what?" I said, intrigued.

"No."

"Did he say why he couldn't see me tonight?" I said, miffed.

"No."

"What about tomorrow during the day? Did he say why he couldn't make it then?"

"No," my mum laughed, exasperated. "I've just told you all the things he said. That was it. Now, we're cooking a vegetarian pasta dish with tofu. Do you want some?"

"No thanks, I've just had some chips," I said,

wondering what Billy was doing and why he couldn't see me.

A new job. I was sure it was. I allowed myself to feel quite pleased for him and I continued on with my notes.

# 8

# The College

East London Sixth-Form College was just at the edge of Epping Forest. I'd arranged to go there just before lunchtime to see Jennifer Ryan's tutor, who was going to introduce me to a couple of her friends and, if he was prepared to see me, the ex-boyfriend.

My mum gave me a lift even though it was slightly out of her way.

"When are you going to put in for your driving test?" she said, as we were going along.

"Definitely as soon as this case is finished," I said.

"You always say that. You're always putting it off."

"When is Gerry going home?" I said, to change the subject.

"I told you, it's for two weeks," she said, her voice a good deal cooler than before. "I thought you said you didn't mind him."

"I don't," I said, "but it's a different thing living with someone."

"He's not exactly living with us. He's just a guest."

"If he could just stop calling me Pats!" I complained.

"Are you saying," she said quietly, "that the only reason he irritates you is because he calls you Pats?"

"Not exactly," I said, my voice sinking down into my neck.

"One day, Patsy, not a million years from now, you're going to leave home. You might get married, you might move into a flat with friends or with Billy. You might move away to another part of the country for a new job. When that happens I'm going to be on my own. Have you considered that?"

"Yes."

"You mustn't begrudge me some company. I know you're not keen on him but it's not you who's going to be spending time with him. It's me."

"Yes," I said, defeated.

Up in front was the sixth-form college and I pulled my rucksack together and pushed my glasses back up my nose. In just over a week Gerry Lawrence would be gone and things would be back to normal.

"Bye, love," my mum called, as the car pulled

away from the curve. A second later I heard a blast of music as she put the radio on.

"I'm Mike Crosby," the man in the dark green suit said, holding his hand out for me to shake. He had striking dark hair that was standing bolt upright on the top of his head. There was a plastic shine to it, suggesting a generous dollop of gel.

"Patsy Kelly," I said, dragging my eyes away from the carefully moulded style. "Thanks for making the time to see me."

He led me through a large atrium which stretched up two floors and ended with a glass roof. There were groups of students everywhere; tall, short, fat, thin, black, white, Asian. They were sitting at tables, lolling about chatting, some juggling balls and one or two couples involved in deep snogging. I tried to avert my eyes. Mike Crosby must have seen me staring and laughed.

"Young love!" he said.

He was older than I'd first thought, about fifty I guessed; the lines around his eyes crinkling up with merriment. He was immaculately dressed with small, round glasses and a vivid green-and-yellow tie. I wondered if, as well as the gel, he occasionally used a little dye, to cover up the grey. I shrugged my shoulders. It wasn't just the young who were allowed to be vain.

I was dressed in a short denim skirt that I'd

recently bought, with thick red tights and a red jumper. On top I had a black leather zip-up jacket that I'd had for a while and a small grey beret which snugly fitted on top of my hair and made it sit quite nicely at the back.

"This is my teaching room, do come in," Mike Crosby said, leading me along to a much quieter part of the college.

I walked into a large, airy classroom. The windows stretched from the ceiling to the floor and there were grey Formica tables, not desks. Instead of a blackboard, there was a white laminate board with an overhead projector standing in front.

"Grab a seat," Mike Crosby said. "I'll just go and get the students."

He disappeared out of the door and I spent some minutes looking at the posters that covered the walls. There were dozens of them, it seemed, all about different aspects of community service. It was then I remembered that Mike Crosby was the teacher who liaised with St Michael's hostel, as well as being Jennifer's tutor. The Big Link: only it had been looked into by the police and dismissed just like the other Big Link, the dentist.

I walked to the front of the room and sat down at the teacher's desk. There was a tidy pile of files all with white rectangular handwritten labels on them. To the side was a small perspex photograph holder in which there was a picture of a smiling woman and two small children. The woman was blonde, quite young-looking, and the children were both under school age. I wondered if it was a photo of Mike Crosby's daughter and grandchildren.

Out of nosiness I tugged at the desk drawers, only to find them locked. Then I sat back and surveyed the classroom. Neat, tidy, no graffiti, no tipped-over chairs and no broken windows. Most of all, none of the *smell* of a regular classroom, the inevitable odour of thirty young, hormonal, hot and bothered teenagers.

Mike Crosby came back a couple of minutes later with two girls who both looked guilty as hell, their foreheads lined, their fingers woven together. One of them was a petite blonde and the other was a small, thin black girl.

"Hi, I'm Patsy Kelly," I said. "I'm not with the police, I'm just checking up on a couple of things."

Mike Crosby told them both to sit down and we proceeded to have a rather one-sided conversation where I seemed to do most of the talking. They kept looking at each other coyly, as though everything I was saying was embarrassing them. *No, they didn't know anything. No, they hadn't heard of Susan Yorke and didn't think that Jenny had known her. No, they'd never been to the homeless hostel.*

After a while, they changed their answers slightly. *Yes, they'd known that Jenny was having dental treatment. Yes, they knew that she and her boyfriend had split up. Yes, he'd been really upset when she'd been killed. Yes, they'd let me know if anything at all came to mind about the murder.*

They went off armed with one of my cards each.

"They're not what you'd call the brightest of students," Mike Crosby said, looking at his watch. "Steven White should be here in a minute. You'll find him quite a different character."

"The police reports said that Jennifer only visited St Michael's twice."

"Yes, she did a bit of decorating work down there, helping to paint a room, I think. She never did any of the evening work, never met any of the clients."

"Why was that?"

"Not all students want that kind of hands-on work. Sometimes they want to keep away from the actual people in the community. We don't force them. It's their choice."

"Might she not have gone there one evening without you knowing about it?"

"I suppose so, but this was all checked out last year. The police had the names of all the students involved. I think it's very unlikely that she went there in the evening."

The classroom door burst open suddenly and a figure stood there. A young man of about eighteen whose hair was bleached almost white and who was wearing a leather biker jacket. In one hand he had his safety helmet and in the other he had a can of Diet Coke.

"Steven," Mike Crosby said, "this is the woman I was telling you about."

Steven White gave me a brief nod, pulled a nearby chair across, turned it round and sat on it in a back-to-front way. All the time he hadn't said a word, just looked at each of us in turn.

I looked at his poise on the chair, the way he was holding his can of drink, his crash helmet held prominently out. Something in the back of my head said "phoney". I got straight to the point.

"Steven, you and Jennifer went out together for some months."

"Yep!" he said brusquely.

"But you broke up a couple of weeks before she died. Can you tell me why?"

I'd read this in the police notes but I wanted to hear him tell it.

"Do I need a solicitor here, sir?" he said, giving Mike Crosby a sideways look.

"No, of course not," he said.

"This is just a chat," I smiled.

"I've heard of friendly chats with the law where people end up incriminating themselves."

"I'm not the law," I said, wondering if he had any reason to incriminate himself.

"Same difference," he said sulkily.

"This young lady," Mike Crosby gave me a

beaming smile, "is just going over the case notes, Steven. She's been hired by the mother of the other dead girl. It's not going to hurt you to help her out."

"We broke up because I was sure that she was seeing someone else. It was a handy excuse, really. We weren't exactly getting on that well. This mate of mine had seen her in a café talking to some bloke. She denied it."

He stretched his arms out and looked like he was going to yawn. He had a bored expression on his face as if he had no feelings about it at all.

"And you didn't see her, on the night that she was killed? Her friends said that she was definitely meeting someone in the Willow Tree."

"It weren't me. Me and her was finished. I don't go out with girls who've got some other bloke in tow. I don't need to. I can go into college and fix up a night out with one of half a dozen better-looking girls than Jennifer Ryan."

"When was the last time you actually saw her?"

"A couple of days before. She was out the front with her mate, Affie."

"Affie?" I said.

"Some kid she knew from her old school. She's not at the college. They were standing chatting and I walked past. This Affie's giving me a long look so I says, 'Don't look at what you can't afford.' Affie just giggles, Jenny pretends to ignore me. Like I said. I weren't bothered." He shrugged his shoulders.

After a few more minutes of the same I handed him one of my cards. He stood up, pushing the chair carelessly away, and left the room like an actor making an exit. I wondered if he had cared at the time.

"I don't think they've been much help," Mike Crosby said, walking across to his desk. I could hear the rattle of his keys as he bent over to open the top drawer. On the crown of his head there was a bald patch the size of a fifty-pence piece.

"They're just confirming the stuff I've already read about the case. I'm really only checking it over. I am interested in this other boyfriend stuff, though."

"The police will have looked into that, I should imagine."

"Yes, I'm sure you're right." I nodded my head. "Would you take my card?" I said. "I've given out more of these in last few days than in all the time I've had them. It's just in case anything occurs to you."

He put the card in his top drawer and began to sort through a pile of papers.

"Nice family," I said, pointing to the photo.

"My wife and our sons," he said, beaming. "Mark is five and James is three and a half."

"Oh?" I said, glad that I hadn't called them his grandchildren.

"We met when she was a student at another

college I taught at. About ten years ago. I tell you," he shook his head, as if remembering something, "marrying a younger woman, it's taken years off me!"

I smiled and noted, under the gel, his receding hairline and the lines across his forehead. How many years were there between him and his wife? Twenty? Thirty, even? It was hard to tell.

It was change-of-lesson time and I had to push and shove my way out of the college. Going through the lower atrium I thought I saw the two girls I'd spoken to earlier, both huddled over a payphone. One of them caught my eye and gave me a friendly wave.

I zipped my jacket up, sidestepped a couple snogging madly by the door and went to look for the bus stop.

The message Billy had left for me said that he wanted me round his house about eight. He was cooking a meal, he said. I made an effort getting ready, putting a silk blouse on and a pair of sparkly earrings. I piled up all the case notes and left them in the corner of my bedroom.

It was a mild evening and I pushed the case to the back of my mind and started to think about Billy and his new job, whatever it was. It would be good for Billy to work with other people, I knew that. Since his parents' deaths he had spent too much time on his own, with me or with broken-down cars.

Not that he needed the money. He wasn't rich, but his parents had left him everything, the house, their insurance, their savings. But having a job wasn't just about money, I knew that. It was about having some self-respect. Seeing yourself in other people's eyes. Doing something useful in the world; making a difference.

He let me in as soon as I knocked. Once in the door I hardly had a moment to take my coat off when he pulled me round and kissed me hard on the lips. My eyes shot open in surprise and his hand on my back made me shiver with pleasure.

The kitchen was a surprise as well. All the lights were out and dotted around the room were candles; on the window sill, on the shelf, on top of the fridge, in the middle of the table.

"What's this in aid of?" I said, half smiling at all the trouble he'd gone to.

"A special treat. Some of it's mine and some I bought from a shop. Get a drink from the fridge and I'll put the starter out. Then I can tell you about the job."

A starter! I sat down bemused and looked at the plate in front of me. A slice of smoked salmon sat there with some dressing on the side. On the edge of the plate were two tiny triangles of brown bread. I started to eat. I was hungry and the dressing and the salmon made my mouth water.

"Tell me about the job," I said, finishing a mouthful.

"The interview took all day. Forty people turned up this morning for some talks and tests and discussion sessions. Then they whittled it down to twenty."

"Where was it?" I said, puzzled. I'd not heard of interviews being on such a large scale before. "Tell me everything. The job, the hours, the pay. I want to know everything."

"It was in an office building in Holborn."

"That's where the job is?" I said.

"Not exactly, no. Like I said, twenty of us went back this afternoon and fifteen got through. I was one of them!"

I'd finished my starter so Billy cleared the plates away and got a tray of lasagne out of the oven. He spooned a great dollop on to my plate and put a stick of garlic bread on the table. My food was steaming, so I broke up the bread and started to nibble mine while he sat down again.

"What exactly will you be doing?"

"Sort of like social work. Working with people who are at risk."

"Social work? You need qualifications for that, surely."

"Not as a social worker, exactly. More like an auxiliary. For example, last year a couple of people worked in a school for the deaf, helping, looking after the students, befriending them, generally supporting them. There's other places, working with the mentally handicapped or people who have been maimed due to war, you know, lost a limb or without a family."

"A war?" I laughed. "It's a long time since we've had a war."

I forked up a mouthful of lasagne and smiled.

"Where will you be based?" I said, still smiling.

"Angola," he said, looking earnestly at me.

I almost nodded and went on without registering his answer. I was about to ask him about the pay and whether there was any training when I stopped.

"Angola?" I said.

"In Africa."

"Oh, that Angola," I said, putting my fork down. "*That* Angola in Africa, you mean. Not the one up the A12, outside Southend?"

"Patsy, don't get upset."

"You've taken a job in Africa?"

"I've tried for other jobs, in this country."

"For about a week. You looked at the papers for a week and you got put off!"

"I'd need a degree, I'd need to go to university."

"What's wrong with that?"

"You didn't want to do it!"

"That was different."

"Why? All I want is a job where I can help people. This job is for a year. A year abroad and when I come back I can carry on working in this field."

"But what about us?"

There was a quiet rage building up inside me. Billy had planned this for days. Had gone to interviews without saying a word to me. Now it was all sewn up.

"You could come with me," he said, softly.

"What do you mean?"

"This is a volunteer job. There's another round of interviews in a month. You could go for a post. We could go together. Think of the experience, Patsy. A year in Africa. It could change our lives."

"I don't want my life changed."

I pushed my plate away, my food untouched.

"It's just a year. It's not like you couldn't take up your job again when you came back, if you wanted."

"What about my mum?"

"Your mum's got Gerry. It's only a matter of time before they get married. Anyone can see that."

*My mum and Gerry getting married?*

"I'm going home," I said, pushing my chair back.

"Patsy, don't be like this." Billy pushed his lasagne away.

I walked out and left him there, sitting in the candlelight.

# 9

# The Dentist

The next morning, I got up before my mum and Gerry and went straight to the office. It was only seven-thirty but I let myself in, put the lights and the heater on and began to make myself a cup of tea.

I was still bristling with rage at Billy. Thoughts inside my head were racing back and forth in unresolved temper. Somewhere deep inside my chest a feeling of hurt was forming. I tried to throw myself into the work. I turned the computer on, read through the case notes, the witness statements. I couldn't help feeling miserable, though. At eight-thirty I rang and arranged to go and see the dentist, Mr Silver, just before lunch.

I kept looking at my mobile phone, half expecting

it to ring, for Billy to laugh and tell me it had only been an idea, a plan, probably something he wouldn't actually go and do. There was no phone call, though, and at ten to nine, when my uncle came in, I was close to tears.

"Patsy, case conference in my office in ten minutes."

"What?" I said, sniffing back the emotion.

"Bring all your notes and ideas in and we can talk it through. A nice cup of tea and some biscuits would be good."

I brightened up, clicked the kettle on and began to sort through my notes.

"Now, you tell me what your strategy was," Tony said, putting his steaming mug of tea to one side.

"Right," I said, in a businesslike way. "I decided that I couldn't go over everything that the police had done, so I thought I would just look over a few areas. The first was the scene-of-crime, the river Lea. I went down there and spoke to a few people, took some photographs, made notes."

"OK," Tony said. He was writing something down.

"Then I went to St Michael's hostel and spoke to the man who works there. I also have a contact there from a previous case, she's going to try and talk to some of the clients."

"Clients?" Tony interrupted, his lip curling.

I carried on. "Then I went to the college that

Jennifer Ryan attended and saw her tutor, a couple of her friends and the ex-boyfriend."

"That it?"

"No, I'm going to see the dentist today. He treated Susan Yorke when she was in the Christmas shelter and he was also treating Jennifer Ryan. That's the other obvious link."

"OK."

Tony took a long sip of his tea and slipped a pink wafer biscuit into his mouth.

"Now go through with me why you've been doing all this."

"Right," I said, shuffling my papers. "The girls were murdered in exactly the same way, in the same place. That strongly suggests one murderer. Statistics show that most people are murdered by someone that they know. The lack of a struggle, or noise, or attempts to run away: all these things suggest that the girls knew their killer. If we can find places or people that are common to both of them, then that could point a strong finger towards who might be responsible."

"So that's the hostel and the dentist?"

"Yes."

"But the police have already followed these up extensively."

"I know. There are two things I'm hoping for. Firstly, that resurrecting the whole thing might jog someone's memory. Something that they hadn't seen as important. Perhaps they'd deliberately kept something back the first time round. Now, a year later they may feel more confident about talking."

"It's a long shot," Tony said.

"I know. The second thing I'm hoping to do is to let the killer know that the investigation is still going on. It may be that I've already spoken to that person. I want to unsettle the killer, maybe push them into contradicting things they said in their original statement, trip them up, who knows? I want to be a sort of irritation."

"I don't think you'll have much trouble there!"

My uncle started to laugh and it took me a minute to realize that he'd made a joke. I gave him a stern look and carried on.

"I've given my cards out to all of the people I've spoken to. That way they have my name and number. I'm really hoping for that bit of forgotten evidence. That all-important clue."

"What if no one comes forward? What if you hear nothing and the two links turn out to be dead ends?"

"Then I'll have to look for another one. Somehow these two girls were linked in some way. That's why they were murdered. It's there, somewhere. The missing link is there somewhere."

The dentist's surgery was in an ordinary semi-detached house. I went in the front door and was alarmed by a shrill bell that went off in my ear. A woman with dark hair and very red lipstick was sitting at a desk speaking to someone on the phone. She had a badge on that said *Sue Wright: Receptionist* and she nodded pleasantly to me and pointed to the chairs.

While I was sitting there the bell buzzed impatiently again and a young man came in with a tray of sandwiches. He had a baseball cap on with the words *Capricorn Sandwiches* across the front and he lumbered across the waiting room and put his tray on the receptionist's counter and waited. He gave me a light smile and I realized then it was almost lunchtime. I got my purse out and bought a tuna mayonnaise on brown bread from him. I was in the course of paying for it when I heard a loud voice singing from one of the back rooms.

The sandwich boy smiled at my surprise.

"That's Mr Silver. He's known round here as the Singing Dentist."

Sue Wright, the receptionist, put the receiver down and smiled at me saying, "Are you Patsy Kelly? Mr Silver will be with you in a moment."

I took my sandwich and tucked it in my rucksack while the sound of "A Hard Day's Night" came into the waiting room. I had a job keeping a straight face but the sandwich boy didn't bat an eyelid.

The sandwich boy left a few minutes later and then Sue Wright started working on the computer.

As well as the sound of singing from the back surgery, I could also hear the high-pitched drone of the drill. I ground my teeth together and decided not to think about how long it had been since I'd had dental treatment.

I began to think about Billy and the phone call he hadn't yet made to me. *Africa*. It was a very long way off. How could he expect me to pack my job in and go with him? I found my lips pursing up and began to wonder when he had first thought of it. How was it that I hadn't noticed his interest. Why hadn't I seen the signs?

And then I thought, what if he had told me? What would I have said? I would have tried to talk him out of it, attempted to persuade him to get a job here or consider a college course. But now I had no chance to persuade him because he had already made up his mind and had been offered the job.

Inside me there was a niggling frustration. We'd been friends for years and for a long time had flirted with each other, sometimes getting together and then quickly backing off. Then recently we'd finally pushed it further and admitted our feelings. For just over four months we'd been a couple: now Billy had made plans to go and spend a year abroad. It was like a slap in the face.

"Miss Kelly?" A loud voice interrupted my thoughts. It was the Singing Dentist.

"Oh." I stood up, aware that I'd been mentally

absent for a few minutes. The patient he'd been treating was standing at the desk, holding his jaw in one hand and his cheque book in the other.

"Why don't you come into the surgery?"

I followed him down a long hallway as he broke into the chorus of "She Loves You". Once in the surgery I floundered about, not knowing where to stand.

"Sit here," he said, pointing to the dentist's chair.

"I'm fine standing," I said, grimacing at the leather reclining chair with the glass of water at its side.

"You're working for Susan Yorke's mother?" he said, getting straight to the point. He sat on a high stool by the side of a computer monitor.

"I am."

"Terrible business," he said, shaking his head. "The police came to see me at the time. I told them everything then."

"I know. I'm just checking over everything," I said, leaning against the side of the chair.

"I work for Crisis. I don't make a big deal about it. I give them maybe six days voluntary work a year, a couple at Christmas, the rest dotted about. I usually go into one of the big hostels and see up to thirty people a day. Most of them are a lost cause. I clean them up a bit, give the odd filling, the odd extraction, nothing bigger, no long-term dental work, you understand. Now and then someone comes with a problem and I really need to see them again."

"Susan Yorke?"

"Yes." He swivelled on his chair and tapped into the computer monitor. A few seconds later the screen was full of information.

"She had an abscess, under her lower left molar. It was giving her a lot of pain at Christmas so I gave her some antibiotics and told her to come and see me about ten days later. She didn't turn up for her appointment but came eventually on the eleventh of February, a Monday, I think. Her appointment was at twelve-fifteen. I cleaned her up, gave her a filling and sent her on her way. Her teeth and gums were suffering from the kind of lifestyle she had. Anyway, after she left I never set eyes on her again."

I nodded, recognizing the details from the police reports. "And Jennifer Ryan?"

He tapped the keyboard again.

"Jennifer Ryan had three appointments; the twentieth of February, the second and twelfth of March. All during her college lunchtime. She had two fillings and a clean up. Nice straight healthy teeth. After she left I didn't see her again. When the murder came out in the papers I didn't actually register the fact that either of them had been here. It was only when the police turned up that I realized that I'd seen both girls."

"And they checked your alibis?"

"With my family on both evenings. My wife and my two teenage sons." He shrugged.

"And you never saw either of them again?"

"Nope," he said and shrugged his shoulders again.

I left the surgery after giving him and Sue Wright a card each, asking them if they could think back to the days in question and contact me if they remembered anything unusual at all. Sue Wright nodded thoughtfully and tucked the card at the edge of the computer monitor. The dentist went back down the hall to his surgery. I could hear him humming loudly, building up to some song or other.

At the bus stop I pulled my sandwich out of my bag and started to eat.

That was it. I'd seen everyone who I'd planned to see. All there was left to do was to work on the report and wait to see if anyone rang with any information.

The road was empty ahead and as far as I could see there were no buses. A sense of anticlimax hit me suddenly. How ridiculous it seemed. I had hoped that someone would suddenly chirp up with something they hadn't told the police a year before. "Oh, yes, I remember I saw both girls with a tall dark man walking along by the river Lea. Oh, yes! That same man bought yards of pink ribbon from a shop just a few weeks before. Oh, yes! That man's name was…"

Across the road I saw the sandwich boy coming out of an office block. His tray was almost empty and he was singing to himself as he walked back to a van that said *Capricorn Sandwiches. Free Delivery*.

I looked at my watch and saw a tiny red dot up ahead on the horizon. The bus that would take me back to the office. I finished off my sandwich, stuck the plastic triangle into my rucksack and waited for it to come closer.

# 10

## Ruffled

Billy finally phoned me the next morning. He was friendly and said that we should talk about it more "when I'd had time to think it through". My voice was clipped and I refused to be jollied into being nice about the whole thing. I did agree to see him for a drink on Saturday night. As far as I was concerned, though, there was nothing to think through. He was going to spend the next year thousands of miles away from me and I could see our relationship disappearing somewhere between the two continents.

I decided to spend Friday in the office getting the case into order. That would mean that I'd worked on it solidly for a week. Was that worth two thousand pounds? I didn't think so. My uncle Tony was more positive, though.

"You've done some legwork. Now sit back and see if anything comes of it. Make a few random phone calls to other witnesses. You might be lucky enough to turn up something."

He was on his way out as he said this. He was dressed in a dark suit and tie and in his hand he had his laptop computer in its case.

"Where's the conference?" I said.

"Canterbury. Long weekend. Food and accommodation provided. Four hundred quid!" he said.

"Four hundred pounds!" I said, immediately irritated. More of Kerry Yorke's money spent.

"It's all tax deductible. I've left the number at which I can be contacted. Only if something urgent comes up, though."

He left a few minutes later and I sat back down at my desk and looked at the pile of files and bits of paper that I had amassed to do with the river Lea murders and felt my heart sink. It sat like a pile of unwanted homework; a maths problem that couldn't be solved; a science experiment that didn't have a conclusion.

I picked up the file of witness statements and had a flick through. The police had taken statements from eighty-two people in total. There were about thirty main statements from the families and friends, the people at the hostel, the dentist's, the college and the scene-of-crime. The rest were loosely related. People who lived near the river Lea, people who had been questioned in a reconstruction that was done the week after Jennifer Ryan's body was found. There were statements from the pub owner, the people in the rowing school, the barge owner who had seen the mystery van. My police inspector friend, Heather Warren, was right. They had been thorough.

I chose four random statements and pushed the rest of the documents away. I walked into my uncle's office and sat on his leather swivel chair, put my feet up and started to read. The first two were from passers-by who used the river walkway as a short cut for work. One was a bus driver and the other a school teacher. They had both passed by the spot where the bodies were found without noticing a thing. The third was a woman who had been walking her dog by the river on February 13th, the night that Susan Yorke had died. She'd seen Susan and a couple of other young people sitting on the bench drinking cans of lager.

The woman had passed by and felt irritated by the young people. She'd also been concerned because it had been bitterly cold and just getting dark. The girl's coat was open and she seemed underdressed. She was laughing, stupidly, and the woman had thought that she'd been drunk. I tried to imagine the scene. Three young homeless people lounging about on the bench near the river. I picked up the photos I had taken the day I had gone down there. I had sat on that very bench, facing the rowing club and backing on to the waste ground.

I pictured a woman walking by with a dog, giving the group of people a hard stare. Perhaps they were quiet while she passed, then burst into laughter, making jokes, drinking more, generally loafing about.

That had been about eight o'clock in the evening. Susan had probably gone into the water about eleven or midnight.

They had carried on drinking for a while and there could have been a row. The other kids going off in a huff and Susan walking off up the river, under the concrete bridge, passing the moored barges. It was difficult to say because the other homeless kids had never come forward. They had never given their side of the story. That's why the police had suspected that Susan's death had been the result of a stupid game that had gone wrong.

Susan Yorke must have ended up walking alone along the river later that night. Perhaps her attacker had walked behind her, in the shadows, waiting until she was too drunk to fight back. Maybe he had befriended her, started up a conversation, then, when no one was looking, had simply pushed her into the water.

No, that wouldn't do. There was the pink ribbon, tied neatly round the wrists, looking pretty and deadly at the same time. All he had to do was shove her in. She couldn't swim. There would be panic for a few seconds, maybe she would call out, but the amount of alcohol she had drunk and the cold water would have quickly put her into shock.

It wouldn't have taken her that long to die.

The fourth statement was that given by Robert Pettifer Wilson, the pub owner. Jennifer Ryan had gone into his pub at about nine-thirty on the night of March 14th. She'd been alone, bought herself a drink and sat down. He'd noticed her because she'd been pretty, attractive, "the way girls ought to look", he'd said. I bristled at this and read on. She'd sat there for about an hour looking at her watch and twice she'd come and asked him if there'd been any phone calls for someone called Jenny. There hadn't been any so she'd sat down again. She'd bought herself one drink after another and seemed very gloomy. She'd clearly been stood up and had been rude to a couple of young lads who had started to talk to her. Eventually she'd left. Robert Pettifer Wilson hadn't been quite sure of the time, about ten-thirty possibly. That was the last he'd seen of her.

In my mind I saw her come out of the bright, noisy pub into the pitch black of the riverside. Had someone followed her out? I looked back at the statement. There'd been about twenty people in there, the landlord had said, some regulars, who he'd named, but also some strangers, "passing trade". No, of course he hadn't noted what they looked like, he was a businessman and had been too busy running a pub. "Course if I'd known in advance that some girl was going to be murdered I'd have taken notes," he said.

For some reason she'd ended up walking along the river. She was worse for wear because of the drink. She was also angry at having been stood up. Had her new boyfriend turned up just at that moment? There may have been a row, during which she stomped off. He could have followed her up the walkway and in a moment of fury pushed her into the water.

But no. There was the pink ribbon to explain.

I sat back and felt my energy drain. If I didn't start typing the report out soon I never would. After a while I went back into my office and started to sort through the paperwork. That was when I noticed, out the corner of my eye, something on the floor just by the door. I looked away, at first thinking it was just a piece of paper that I'd dropped. It kept catching my attention, though, irritating me, so I went over and picked it up.

It was an envelope, addressed to me, *Miss Patsy Kelly*. The words were typed neatly.

Where had it come from? I stood in the middle of the office holding it stupidly. I hadn't heard anyone push anything under the door. When had it appeared? Recently? When I'd been in Tony's office reading the statements?

The quiet became noticeable, heavy even. I stepped

across, opened the door and looked out. The stairwell light was off so I leaned out of the doorway and clicked it on. The stairway was empty and the street door at the bottom was closed. A tiny worry was uncurling inside my chest. I tore open the envelope. Inside was a typewritten note.

*PATSY KELLY. If you want to find out more about the murders go down to the Waterside bench tonight after dark. Come alone. No police or no deal.*

I read it over, three, four times. Then I turned straight to the window and looked up and down the street outside. There was no one unusual, just regular people doing their shopping, on their way home from work.

Someone had come up to the office and slipped this under the door while I was inside. I felt a tiny prick of excitement. Could it be that someone I had spoken to actually had some information that they wanted to give me? Someone who wanted to remain anonymous?

I began to pack up my things hurriedly, shoving my papers into my rucksack. It was almost five by the time I'd finished. I turned the computer off and put the answerphone on. I locked the office door and took the stairs two at a time. When I stepped out of the street door it was beginning to get dark.

I pulled the note out and looked hard at it again.

Was it a serious note? I wondered. A hoax maybe? I stood for a minute unsure how to proceed. And then something unpleasant occurred to me. Could the note be from the killer?

I didn't know who it was from and there was only one way to find out. I had to go down to the river Lea after dark. I was certain of one thing, though, I wasn't going alone.

# 11

# After Dark

Billy answered the door as soon as I knocked. I followed him into the kitchen and found the table covered in leaflets and books about Africa. There was a half-finished cup of coffee and a set of forms that he'd been in the process of filling in.

"You're applying for a passport?" I said.

"You wouldn't believe it but I don't have one. I've never needed one. You know me, I've never travelled beyond England."

"Right," I said, thinking that Africa was too far to go for a first trip abroad.

"I thought we weren't meeting until tomorrow?" he said, looking hopefully at me.

I realized then that he thought I had changed my mind about working abroad. I was mildly irked.

"I need your help with the case," I said. "I've got to go somewhere and I need someone with me."

His face dropped. "You mean you need a lift?"

"No, more than that," I said, realizing that it hadn't come out the way I had intended.

"Come on," he said, drinking his coffee down. "I haven't got that long, I'm going to a meeting with some co-workers tonight."

"We won't be long," I said, "an hour or so. That's a promise!"

I grabbed his arm playfully but he shook me off and walked ahead of me up the hallway. I put my hands in my pocket and followed him. It was no time for a row.

We didn't speak all the way there. Eventually after what seemed like hours of silence I told him what we were going for. I spoke in a light-hearted voice and said that I'd had a tip off that there might be some information down at the scene of the crime. I tried to cover up my excitement with a careless attitude as if I didn't really expect to find anything. That way I wouldn't look foolish if it turned out to be a hoax.

It was completely dark as we drove off the main road to the Willow Tree pub. The car park was on uneven ground and we went forward slowly and awkwardly. There were fewer lights as we faced the river and the waste ground that mainly surrounded it. It was much quieter as well, even though the rush-hour traffic was only a couple of hundred metres behind us.

"Thanks again," I said, to break the silence, "this'll only take about ten minutes, then you can be on your way. I can get a bus home. You go straight to your meeting."

"There's no need for that," he said. "I've got to go back home and pick up the paperwork."

*Paperwork.* I found myself groaning inwardly. Billy now had a job to go to, people to meet up with and *paperwork* to look at. Soon he would be telling me all the statistics of third world poverty and showing me maps of where he was going to go. I looked sideways at him. The arm nearest to me was holding on to the top of the steering wheel and seemed to be dividing his bit of the car off from mine. There was no warmth between us, no connection. It was all because of his new job and it wasn't fair.

"I don't know why you're in such a mood with me," I said. "I only asked you to help me out. It's not as if it's going to take very long, after all."

"I've come, haven't I?" He turned to me, his face full of anger. "I've dropped what I was doing to take you on some very important piece of investigative work."

I was stung by his tone of voice. I tried to ignore it, keeping the case uppermost in my mind. *If you want to find out more about the murders go down to the*

*Waterside bench…* If there was something there then it might be the kick-start that the case needed.

"I know, I'm sorry," I forced myself to say. I opened the car door and held it there for a minute.

"Sorry?" he said, not sounding in the least bit assuaged. "That's it, though, isn't it? Your job comes first, doesn't matter what I want."

"That's not true," I said, putting one leg out of the car. It was dark, it was the river Lea, I had a bench to go and look at and I was having trouble keeping my temper down.

"Oh, walk away when you don't want to talk about it."

"I'll tell you what, Billy," I said, in my most measured voice, "you go on home and I'll manage from here. You go to your meeting about saving the world. Meanwhile I'll just try and sort out a couple of murders."

That set him off.

"You? Sorting out a couple of murders? Patsy, anybody with half a brain could see that this isn't going to go anywhere. You're just passing time. None of it will make the slightest difference to one single solitary person."

"To Kerry Yorke?" I raised my voice.

"Her daughter's dead, Patsy. Nothing you can do will bring her back."

I closed the car door and walked around to his side. I counted to ten in my head.

"Thanks for the lift, Billy. I'll be fine now. We can talk about all this when we're both a bit calmer."

He had a look of frustration on his face. He wanted to argue with me, I knew, but I wasn't rising to it. He looked straight into my eyes for a few seconds, then he seemed to make a decision. His expression said, *if that's the way you want it...* and he turned the ignition on and put the car into reverse.

I watched him screech out of the car park and join the traffic. I stood for a moment, flapping both my arms at my sides like a disorientated bird. Then I realized that in my rush to get out of the car I'd left my rucksack behind. I stamped my foot with annoyance. I patted my leather jacket and felt my mobile phone in my pocket. In my jeans pocket I felt a pound coin. Bus fare. It was better than nothing.

I turned and walked round the pub and stood in the light that spilled out of its windows. The river path was ahead of me, dotted with miniature street lamps. I could see the concrete bridge and the moored barges. Just beyond, round a bend, was the Waterside bench.

It was six-thirty and, although it was dark, there were several people walking to and fro on either side of the river. *Aquarius Foods* was open and I could see Alan and Ian Payne serving and three men in overalls standing drinking cups of steaming liquid. I wondered if Alan Payne had shown my card to customers as he'd said he would. I pulled my coat round my shoulders, tensing from the cold, and thought about buying a hot drink.

I didn't. I walked slowly on towards the bridge that was covered in graffiti. I had to stand back to let four people pass me on cycles and I found myself looking at a couple of teenagers kissing breathlessly on the other side of the river. I looked at them and thought of Billy tearing away in his car and wondered what was happening to my romance.

I got as far as the bridge and stopped.

I stood looking under it for a few moments, feeling apprehensive. I remembered my resolution not to go alone. I hadn't intended to, I had arranged for Billy to be with me but it had all gone wrong. The bench was only a couple of hundred metres away and yet, for what must have been a couple of minutes, I stood by the dark river unable to go on. Eventually I made myself walk forward.

Only one bulb under the bridge was working. It gave a veil of eerie light and I trod carefully, afraid that I might slip on the muddy ground. The columns threw their shadows into my path and I put my hands out in front of me in case I collided with one of them. I could see, further up the path, the shape of the moored barges and the bench that I had sat on that first day. It was a few metres away from one of the pathway lights. I put out my foot to carry on but something stopped me. There was a figure, behind the bench, fiddling with something. The person was in darkness and all I could see was an outline. I went to move forward but a ringing bell made me jump and a cyclist whooshed past me and into the semi-darkness.

When I looked again the figure had gone.

I scanned the riverside up and down but could see nothing. The person had slipped away into the darkness. I walked quickly out from under the bridge, the red light from the rear of the cycle winking on and off up in front of me. The barges were locked up and in darkness. When I got to the bench there was definitely no one there. Across the river was the rowing club and I could see some distant lights and a couple of people working over an upside-down boat.

Leaning against the leg of the bench was a padded envelope. I picked it up, looking round all the time. I sat down on the bench and pulled at the fastening. Across the way the rowers were working on the hull of the boat and there was music coming from a radio somewhere near them. I gently put my hand inside the envelope and pulled out a piece of paper. As it came out I felt something else. When my hand emerged there were tendrils of pink ribbon laced across my fingers.

I sat stock still for a moment. The music and the voices faded as I let my fingers fidget in the tangle of shiny pink ribbon. Somewhere underneath was a piece of paper. I looked up again, sure that the men across the way had noticed my shock, my stillness, but their heads were bent. I looked up and down. The river that had seemed so busy a couple of moments before now seemed uncomfortably empty. In the far distance I could see someone walking their dog, but that was all.

I turned the piece of paper over. On it, typed out, was, PATSY KELLY. DEATH BY DROWNING. YOU'RE NEXT.

They were only words on a piece of paper but I was knocked back for a few seconds. DEATH BY DROWNING. I couldn't help but read over it, letting my eyes stray away towards the river, looking thick and oily, barely a ripple of current running through it. I screwed the paper up in a ball and put it into my jacket pocket. Then I shoved the ribbon back into the envelope, my back muscles tensing and knotting together.

It had become darker all of a sudden. The sky was coal black and the walkway lights seemed like tiny candles. I noticed the cold penetrating my jeans and chilling my neck and hands. My breath was making small clouds in the air. I had to get away from the river and back into a warm lit-up place.

The men across the way lifted their heads, finally noticing me.

I took long strides past the moored barges and back towards the bridge. There were no cyclists, no walkers, no one around at all. Because of the bend I couldn't even see the lights of the pub or the café up ahead.

I put my head down and walked boldly under the bridge. It was just a few metres until I got into the yellow light from the lone bulb.

I didn't hear the footsteps. I didn't hear anything. Halfway under that bridge I came to an abrupt stop, as if my legs had turned to liquid and I simply couldn't go on. All there was was the sound of someone breathing heavily behind me.

For that moment, that microsecond, I stood stiller than I've ever been in my life. A frozen figure; the only noise was the thumping of my own heart and the rasping breaths behind me.

I couldn't turn round. I just felt my teeth biting hard into my bottom lip.

Then a pair of strong hands took hold of my shoulders and pushed me hard towards the icy river.

# 12

# Not Waving But Drowning

The cold from the water was like an electric shock which surged through me as I splashed in.

I must have curled up into a foetal shape and plummeted straight to the bottom of the murky river. Strangely, my eyes remained open but could see nothing, just blackness closing in around me. My feet touched the bed of the river, and I pushed against it with my weight, my arms still pinioned to my sides with fright. I must have moved up a metre or so but my clothes seemed to be against me; soaking with water, they pulled me back down.

For a moment I stayed like that, as if hanging in deep space, not sure which way to go. Inside my chest the breath was all gone and my coat hung around my shoulders like a straitjacket.

I knew then that I would die if I didn't do something.

I kicked out at the river bed three, four times and rose up through the sludgy water. I moved my arms out and made powerful swimming movements. I must have risen through the blackness because all of a sudden my head popped out of the water and I splashed around, sucking the air in and coughing at the same time. One of my hands hit my face and knocked against my glasses, which had stayed on.

The river bank was deserted. I splashed out, moving my arms in a swimming motion, opening my mouth in a faint cry and swallowing water at the same time. I turned my head and saw the distant lights of the pub and the café. On the other side there was darkness; behind me, round the bend, the boat-yard, the men working with the radio on. I cried out again, a slurred yell that I knew wasn't going far.

The water in my clothes felt like lead and it was as much as I could do to keep afloat. I knew that it wouldn't be long before I was dragged under again, my breath and my strength being no match for the river. I took a deep breath, thinking that it might be my last, and let out a yell that came all the way from my feet and up through my lungs like a foghorn.

"HELP HELP HELP HELP ME HELP ME!" I cried.

Sinking wearily back into the water I saw some movement at the corner of my eye, and vaguely heard the sound of voices and footsteps getting louder as they came towards me.

Along the river bank were the faces of three men. Their mouths were moving but I couldn't hear what they were saying. I saw a lifebelt being thrown and I made some clumsy movements towards it. I had no strength left but I splashed around, lunging myself in the direction of the lifebelt until I felt its rubbery surface in my hand.

They pulled me towards them, lifted me out of the water and sat me on the concrete ground. A puddle immediately formed around me. I felt dazed, weak, on the edge of a great well of tears. I couldn't speak, couldn't even say "Thank you".

Their voices were full of excitement.

"Lost your footing, love?"

"They should mend them lights."

"Good thing you had your wits about you!"

"You never even lost your glasses!"

A man with a blanket came running towards us and knelt down to put it round my shoulders. It was Alan Payne from the café. The blanket became immediately damp, drawing the water out of my clothes like a magnet. Even though I was soaking wet, sitting in the cold night air I felt oddly warm. The men were being cheerful, laughing and trying to get me to relax.

"I'll ring for an ambulance on my mobile," Alan Payne said.

"No!" I said, my voice sounding more like a croak. "No, there's no need. I'm not hurt, just shaken up. Ring my home number. My mum'll come for me."

I needed to go home, to be alone. I'd have to contact the police, I realized that, but not until I was warm and dry and in my own home. Someone had just tried to kill me, I knew that. I also knew, with a sinking heart, that I would be in trouble with everyone for going on my own, for walking carelessly into a dangerous situation. I had to go home and think it all through before I faced anyone.

Two of the men helped me up and walked me towards the pub, squelching along, leaving a trail of wet behind me. I told Alan Payne my home number and remembered my own mobile. I felt inside my pocket and realized, with dismay, that it had gone, fallen out into the river. Then I remembered the envelope with the pink ribbon. It, too, was gone. All of them lying on the spongy river bed just as I might have been.

"Your mum's out but your dad's coming for you," Alan Payne said.

He meant that *Gerry* was coming to get me. I groaned, thinking about what I was going to say to him.

Inside the pub I sat next to a radiator and was hastily given another dry blanket and a steaming cup of hot, sweet tea by a friendly woman. Over by the bar I could see Robert Pettifer Wilson giving me a stern look. No doubt he thought that my presence would be bad for business. I sipped the tea, looking blithely round the bar at the astonished faces of the drinkers. When the cup was taken from me I felt fatigue finally creeping up on me. I laid my head back and closed my eyes.

Gerry drove my mum's car carefully back through the streets.

"Your mum won't be in until late," he said.

"Promise me you won't tell her about this," I said, for the tenth time. "She'll only worry and it was an accident, after all."

"If you're absolutely sure," he said. "I don't want her worried over nothing."

"Right," I said. For once I was pleased with Gerry's easygoing attitude.

"This seat will be soaked through," I said.

"It'll dry," Gerry said, and patted me delicately on the knee.

Once inside the house he helped me up the stairs and into the bathroom. He turned the shower on and pulled out a couple of big bath towels. When he left I peeled the clothes off, item by item, and left them on the floor, a sopping mess. I stood under the hot water and let it run until I was completely surrounded by a cloud of steam. Then I put my dressing gown on and sat on the floor of the bathroom.

*Someone had tried to kill me.*

113

A bubble of nausea rose in my throat and my hands clasped each other. Someone had slid a note under the office door to make me go to the river Lea after dark. The envelope, the ribbon, the warning, had been put there to scare me. In the end I had gone alone, telling no one the absolute truth, thinking that I could handle the situation.

*How could I have been so foolish?*

The person had known where the office was, had known my name, had known that I was investigating the case. It had been one of the people I had spoken to, someone to whom I'd given my card, *Patsy Kelly, Investigative Work, Good Rates*.

I'd said to Tony that I'd wanted to unsettle the killer, push them into contradicting things they'd said in their original statement. I'd done more than that. After a year during which the investigation had fizzled out I'd opened it up again and someone that I'd spoken to over the last few days hadn't liked it.

I'd given my card to almost a dozen people. They'd all taken it in a kind of bemused way, although one or two – the college girls, the receptionist at the dentist's – had been quite impressed. One of them had pocketed it thoughtfully, though, perhaps planning right from that moment to do something about me. I'd been like a kid poking my finger into a beehive.

I looked at the pile of my clothes. My leather jacket lay across them like a wet animal, shiny and heavy with damp, the lining a soggy mess. It was ruined. I wouldn't be able to wear it again.

My throat became hot and dry and my eyes glazed over and I started to cry. One blink and the tears were running down my cheeks, stopping mid-way as if hanging by a thread until I wiped them away with the back of my hand.

I wasn't crying for the leather jacket or the wet clothes or the fact that a number of people would be mad at me. They were tears of sheer relief that I was sitting there, clean and dry and alive when I could have been lying, cold and dead at the side of the river. I pulled my knees up to my chest and hugged them. Next day the headline might have been KID DETECTIVE IS NUMBER THREE IN RIVER LEA MURDERS.

I remembered something then and lifted my leather jacket up. In the left-hand pocket was the soggy note. I put it on the floor in front of me, gently smoothing it out. The outline of the writing was still visible. PATSY KELLY. DEATH BY DROWNING. YOU'RE NEXT. I looked at it for a while and thought about the people to whom I'd given my card.

One of them was the killer of Susan Yorke and Jennifer Ryan.

# 13

## Tanya

The next day was Saturday, so I didn't bother to get up early. From my bedroom I could hear my mum and Gerry having breakfast so I stayed upstairs. I considered ringing my uncle Tony at the hotel in Canterbury but I couldn't face telling him how reckless I'd been. I imagined him taking a giant sigh and rolling his eyes to other grey-suited businessmen around, saying something like, "She's only twenty, what can you expect?"

I got dressed and waited until my mum and Gerry went out shopping before I went downstairs and had some toast. Then I rang Heather Warren to tell her what had happened. I knew she, perhaps more so than my uncle, would tell me off for going to the river Lea on my own. I also knew I could trust her to do the right thing. I had her direct number. A man answered. I told him who I was and asked to speak to Heather.

"Inspector Warren is attending a crime prevention conference in central London today. Can I be of assistance?"

"When will she be back?" I said.

"I believe it's a whole day course. She's not due into the office until Monday morning. Can I take a message?"

"No, thanks anyway," I said and put the phone down. I would have to wait until the evening. I had her home number and I didn't think she would mind if I rang her there. Until then I would have to think through the case.

I got a new notepad out of my wardrobe and started to make a list of the people I had seen so far in the investigation. I'd spoken to people at the river itself, the hostel, the college and the dentist's. In all, there were about ten names: Robert Pettifer Wilson, Roger Dawkins, any passers-by at *Aquarius Foods* (I made a note to ask Alan Payne if anyone had taken an interest); then there was Peter Lee at the hostel and anyone that Alice had spoken to; at the college was Mike Crosby and the two guilty-looking girls and Steven White the ex-boyfriend; lastly was the singing dentist and his receptionist.

After a while of toying with it all I went up to my bedroom and sat on the bed, my feet under the duvet. I made myself remember the row that Billy and I had had. I let it play over in my head and found myself getting annoyed again at the things that had been said. The anger crumbled, though, when I thought about what might have happened afterwards. A silly row that had led me to walking off into the dark night and almost getting killed.

And anyway, in the scale of things, what did the row matter? Billy was my closest friend. He would be the one person I could talk to about what had happened. I decided to give him a call.

The phone rang three times and then his answer-machine came on. My shoulders dropped with disappointment but I left a message anyway, asking him to ring me as soon as possible. I replaced the receiver just in time for it to start ringing again.

I picked it up. "Hello? Patsy Kelly speaking."

"Patsy, it's me, Alice. I couldn't get through on the mobile so I thought I'd try you at home."

"Right," I said, remembering the mobile sitting at the bottom of the river like sunken treasure.

"I've found a kid who says she was a friend, quite a close friend, of Susan Yorke." Alice sounded breathless.

"Really?" I said.

"Yes, she's a timid kid but very nice. I'm sure she'll talk to you. I've told her to come back about lunchtime."

"I'll be there," I said, looking at my watch. It was just before eleven o'clock.

I found an old shoulder bag in the cupboard and threw some things into it. The note, now stiff and dry, I carefully folded and put into the small zip pocket. I brushed my hair up into an elastic band and put a grey woolly hat on. I put some moisturizer on my skin, which still felt tight and grimy from its dip in the river. Then I went downstairs and out of habit opened the cupboard under the stairs to get out my leather jacket. It wasn't there, though, and I remembered that it was sitting in a damp heap in the bin. I pulled out a zip-up sports jacket that I'd had for a few years and put it on. It didn't go with the hat and I was about to take it off when I thought, *who cares?*

Peter Lee let me into the hostel and pointed me towards the kitchen where Alice was. He was wearing a blouson jacket with jeans and trainers. His designer stubble was still noticeable. He gave me a half-smile, as though he was expecting me but didn't quite approve of the fact that I was there. I couldn't help but look closely at him and remember the night before. He didn't seem to notice my interest, turning away from me immediately and going up a narrow staircase to the floor above.

Alice was sitting down across the table from a girl of about sixteen. She got up as soon as I arrived.

"Patsy, this is Tanya, the girl I told you about."

Tanya looked over the top of a steaming cup of something. I noticed that she still had her coat and gloves on, even though she was in a hot kitchen. I pulled my hat off and sat down.

"Tea?" Alice said and I nodded.

Tanya had ginger hair that sprang off the sides of her head and got lost into a mess of tiny curls. Her face was a pale, creamy colour and she had hundreds of freckles as though someone had flicked a paintbrush at her. She had a nose-ring and a silver stud just above her eyebrow. At her feet, curled up, its nose resting on its tail, was a brown dog.

Alice put the tea in front of me and I glanced at my watch. It was still only twelve-thirty. Hours before I would be able to speak to Heather Warren.

"You seem preoccupied, Patsy," Alice smiled.

"Just a bit," I said, and turned to Tanya. "You knew Susan Yorke?"

"Yes, we was mates. Up to the Christmas, at least. We had a row, though, and I moved on down to Bath."

"So you weren't here when she was killed?"

"No. I didn't even know about it until a couple of months after it happened."

"I don't understand," I said. How could she not know about the river Lea murders?

"Why don't you let Tanya tell it from the beginning, Patsy?" Alice gave me a stern look.

"OK." I put on a smile and sat back. My mind was wandering back and forth, though, thinking about Heather Warren, the night before, the row with Billy, the list of suspects I had.

The girl, Tanya, started uncertainly. "I met Susie here, one night about a month before Christmas. She was nice, I liked her. It was before I had Tiggy."

The dog, Tiggy, looked up at the sound of his name.

"We used to hang around together. She was all right, Susie was. She shared stuff, like if she had some money and I didn't, she'd buy me a bacon roll or a drink and I did the same. We hung around for a few weeks."

"Tell Patsy about the other hostel," Alice said, looking hard at me.

"We always tried to get here about six, so that we had a definite chance of getting in. This particular night, I got held up and we was late. She was annoyed at me, I knew, and when we got here and Peter said the hostel was all full up she had a right go at me. I felt awful and we stood about outside arguing about it. That's when this blue car pulled up and this guy leant across."

I drank my tea in silence, getting more interested in the story she was telling.

"He rolled the car window down and I was about to walk over but Susie stopped me. 'What do you want?' she shouted. The bloke got out of his car and came over to talk to us. 'I know where there's this other hostel,' he said, 'there's always places there. I know for a fact,' he said, 'that there's rooms going there tonight.'"

"What did he look like?" I interrupted.

"Let her finish, Patsy," Alice said.

"Susie said, 'We're not getting in your car, mate, whatever you say.' This bloke, he smiles and pulls out a ten-pound note and scribbles an address down on this bit of paper. 'The closest tube is Hammersmith,' he says. 'Here's the fare and the address. There are empty rooms there. It's up to you whether you use them or not.'"

"'Hammersmith?' I said. It was right over the other side of London.

"So we went over there, on the tube. We found the place and we stayed there. It was the best hostel either of us had ever been in. No, more than that, it was like a hotel. Single rooms, shower and toilet. Matching duvets and curtains and even your own telly in every room. They were single rooms but me and Susie we slept in one together. She knew that I didn't like being on my own."

"Tell Patsy what happened after you'd stayed there a few days."

"It was too good to be true. I said that at the time but Susie just shrugged it off. 'We might as well use it,' she said, 'make the most of it.' Anyway, we saw the bloke, the one who was in the car. He came up to our room and asked us if everything was all right. Like I said, it was like a hotel. Not like any other hostel I've ever seen."

"What was it called, this place?"

"It didn't have a name. It was just this big three-storey house with iron railings in front of it. We were never sure who else was staying there. We saw a couple of girls going in and out but they never spoke to us. It was in a posh area as well, loads of expensive cars around. The bloke, Mickey his name was, he said to be very quiet when we came home late at night so that we didn't disturb anyone."

"Was it owned by an organization?"

"She's coming to that," Alice said, giving Tanya a pat on the shoulder.

"One night, after we'd been there about a week, this bloke Mickey comes up and asks us if we'd like to make a bit of money. He brings this great big box of chocolates and shows us this wad of twenty-pound notes. He asks us if we like the room and whether we'd like to stay there permanently. Susie gets suspicious right away and asks him what kind of work. This Mickey, he opens the chocolates and says, 'Look, girls, I've got a few friends, older men, really nice blokes and sometimes they like to spend a bit of time with a pretty young girl.'"

I must have made a sound because Tanya stopped talking. Alice looked at me and gave me the slightest of nods.

" 'What do you mean?' Susie says. This Mickey, he says, 'All I want you to do is spend a bit of time with these men. Be nice to them. Make them happy for a few hours. Then you can stay here rent free and you'll have some pocket money as well.' "

*Pocket money.* The word brought with it a rush of memories from the past. A couple of pound coins on the dressing-table; comics, sweets, tiny toys. Later on it was make-up and CDs. Tanya was still speaking.

"Me and Susie, we weren't born yesterday. Susie said to him, 'We might be homeless, mate, we might have lost everything but we haven't come to that. Come on, Tanya,' she said, 'get your stuff.' Half hour later we walked out of there. Susie said we were never going back. Funny thing was that, while he was sitting there, this Mickey, Susie swiped the box of chocolates, just took them from in front of him and shoved them into her bag. Then we left."

Tanya was speaking animatedly and smiling widely. Tiggy sat up and started to scratch himself.

"Where did you go then?"

"Back on the streets. We spent a few nights here. Then it was nearly Christmas and we went to the Crisis shelter. Susie had this really bad toothache and she was miserable a lot of the time. We had this row over nothing really but she ended up hanging round with these other kids. When the Christmas shelter closed down I had nowhere to go. I hung around for a while and met these kids who were going down to some place near Bath. A sort of camp, you know, loads of people in tents and caravans. They said I could go with them. That's where I got Tiggy."

We all looked at the dog who cocked his ears and yawned.

"That's how come I never knew that Susie was dead. This camp, it was in some woods south of Bath. We lived there for months; no newspapers, no TVs, hardly any contact with the outside world. When I got back and found that Susie was dead I didn't know what to do. I thought if I came forward, you know, my mum would find out and I'd have to go back home."

"What about Susie, did you ever hear anything about what happened to her, after you left?"

Tanya looked at Alice.

"Tell her," Alice said.

"I can't be sure, it's just what I heard so I don't know how true it was."

"Yes?"

"I heard that she went back to the house in Hammersmith."

I sat silent for a minute and let it sink in. The house in Hammersmith. Mickey, the man who ran it. Being *nice* to his older men friends.

"Have you got the address?" I said.

"No, but I know where it is. I could take you there."

There was a noise from behind me and Peter Lee came into the room. He had an unlit cigarette in his hand.

"This is against the rules, Alice. You know we don't allow clients in here during the day."

"It's OK, Mr Lee," I said, standing up, "we're just leaving."

Alice rolled her eyes at me and I took Tanya by the arm and led her towards the door.

"I'll be back tonight," she said to Alice.

"Make sure you get here on time," she said. "You know how quickly we fill up."

"I'll make sure she gets back," I said, and closed the heavy security door behind me.

# 14

# The House at Hammersmith

I paid Tanya's fare on the tube and bought her a burger and chips which she ate gratefully while Tiggy watched every mouthful. Sitting on the tube she started to tell me why she'd left home.

"My mum was the problem. Everything had to be just right for her. Me and my brother, we had to get up in the morning and make our beds and tidy our rooms, then she came and inspected them. If they weren't right, if like the sheet was sticking out or there was a wrinkle she would make us do it all over again."

I didn't say anything but it didn't seem reason enough to leave home.

"My brother got on her nerves most. She was always comparing him to me and saying that he was useless. She said he was dirty and untidy and didn't care about himself. She said he was stupid and would never get any exams. And when he didn't do his homework she would lock him in his bedroom all evening. She'd use an actual key and lock the door so that he couldn't leave the room, not to go to the toilet or anything."

"What about your dad?" I said.

"My dad seemed to live in a different world. He either didn't notice or he ignored it."

"Is your brother still there?"

"No. It was my brother who went first, about two years ago. He was sixteen and he told me if he didn't go he might do himself some harm. I gave him all my savings. I emptied my building society book; ninety-two pounds. She was furious, didn't speak to me for two weeks. Then she started cross-examining me. *Did I know where he'd gone, did I have an address*, all that stuff. I stayed for another couple of months, until I got some money together. Then I left. I knew that my brother had come to London so I followed him here. I don't know, I suppose I thought it would be easy to find him. I went through all the hostels and the MISSING agencies but I've never seen or heard anything about him. For all I know he might have gone back home!"

She gave me a half-smile and then she leant down and gave her dog a loving stroke.

"You and Susan became friends really quickly,

then?" I said.

"Yes, it's a bit like that when you live on the streets. You meet someone, you get on with them, you stick around together. When we met we found out, almost straight away, that our star signs were compatible. That was important, you know. It was fate."

I remembered what Kerry Yorke had said about Susan's obsession with horoscopes. I also remembered Benny Gold and the rows they had.

"Did she ever talk about why she left home?"

"Not much. I know she hated her mum's boyfriend. She wasn't keen on talking about him. I know one thing, though."

"What?"

"When I last saw her, at Christmas, she told me she was going to go home. She said she'd had enough of living on the streets. She carried this photo of her mum around with her. She missed her, I know she did."

"But why didn't she go?" I said, exasperated.

"You can't." Tanya shook her red curls at me. "Once you've left, it's like, like a statement, you're taking a sort of stand against them. If you go back, it's admitting defeat. It's like saying that you couldn't handle it and you were wrong for leaving in the first place. Listen, there've been times when I haven't had anything to eat in two days. Times when I woke up to find my sleeping bag wet where the rain had soaked through. Times when groups of skinheads followed me through the dark streets calling me names and throwing stones. I've wanted to go back. If only to see if my brother's there. But I can't do it."

The train rumbled along and I thought about Kerry Yorke. If she knew that Susan had wanted to go home, would it make her feel any better? I wasn't sure.

We got out at Hammersmith and walked for about eight minutes. I had my notepad out and was jotting down directions.

"It's just a few turnings along," Tanya said. Tiggy was following us, wagging his tail and sniffing at garden walls and lampposts.

"Did you recognize any of the other girls in the house? I mean, were they kids who might have been living on the street?"

"Don't know. How can you tell? Once someone's got the cash they buy clothes, have their hair done, put make-up on. Who's to say whether they've been on the streets or not?"

I nodded. She was right. We turned the corner of Dodds Street and were faced with a row of about ten three-storey Georgian houses that faced on to a tiny children's park. We walked along and Tanya pointed to number eight.

"That's it," she said.

The front door opened just at that moment and I

linked Tanya's arm and walked on, turning to cross the road a few metres on. I looked around and saw two women come out, whispering quietly together. They were both dressed conservatively; one had a trouser suit on and the other a long coat with a silk scarf. They looked like young businesswomen or professionals, not what I had expected. I wondered whether, after all that time, Tanya had got the right house.

We crossed the road and walked along to the entrance of the park. It was four-thirty and time was getting on. I wasn't sure how to proceed at all. Should I go up to the house and knock on the door, to see who owned it?

Tanya tied Tiggy to the railings and we went inside and sat down on a tiny climbing frame and looked across the road at the house.

"We were up on the second floor at the back," she said. "Our window overlooked some tennis courts. Me and Susie, we said we were going to learn how to play tennis when we got somewhere to live. Keep fit, see?"

She gave me a half-smile and I looked across at the house. Just by the front door I could see a panel of bells with small labels beside them. It looked as though the house was divided up into six dwellings. The door opened then and a middle-aged man in a suit and mac came out. He stood for a moment, adjusting his tie. Then he pulled the door shut behind him and walked on. Tanya looked at me, her eyebrows raised slightly.

"It could be someone who lives there," I said, glumly. "How can we tell?"

I sat there looking at the house for a few more minutes, then I made a decision.

"There's nothing we can do here. We've got the address and your evidence. That should be enough for the police to get a search warrant."

"The police?" Tanya said, looking startled. "Alice never said nothing about the police."

"What are you afraid of? They're not going to ask you about yourself. They're not interested in you!" I said it wearily and then realized that I'd spoken an all too unpalatable truth. Nobody was interested in Tanya. She looked forlorn.

"I don't like getting involved with the police. And anyway, if I go with you to the police I'll lose my place at St Michael's. The police'll keep me for hours and then I won't be able to get in anywhere."

"You could come home with me," I said, without thinking.

"I don't want charity, Patsy. I want to go to the hostel."

"Will you at least come with me in the morning? You can just tell them your name is Tanya. You don't have to give them any other information on yourself. This could be important. This house, it could open the case up again."

"In the morning?"

"Please."

I was about to go on when I noticed Tanya's eyes swivelling from one end of the street to the other. A blue car was pulling up outside the house, double parking in the road, so that a taxi that was behind it beeped loudly.

"What?" I said, looking at her and then back at the car and the irate taxi driver. It was a BMW, small but sleek and its windows were smoked.

"That's the car," she said. "That's the one, I'm sure. I remember the dark windows."

I looked back. The driver had switched his hazard lights on and they were blinking on and off as the other cars manoeuvred round him. He had got out and was bending over to lock the door. Then he stood up and gave the taxi driver a glare and his mouth opened and closed while some angry words came out. I didn't catch what he said above the noise of the traffic. I did catch his face, though. Just twenty metres or so away from him I recognized his stiff dark hair and tailored suit.

"That's the guy. That's Mickey, the man who asked us to work in the hostel!" Tanya said, eagerly.

It was Mike Crosby. The teacher from Jennifer Ryan's college.

# 15

# The Police

After leaving Tanya back at the hostel I decided to go and see Heather Warren straight away. I was hoping that she'd be in and I was very keen to tell her about the house in Hammersmith. I'd visited her once before after a successful case and I was sure she wouldn't mind me calling on her at home.

Mike Crosby had been the man who directed Susan and Tanya to the house in Hammersmith. Mike Crosby, the co-ordinator of community studies at the sixth-form college. He was the one who said they could live there permanently if they were *nice* to some of his older men friends.

It was something that linked him directly to both of the dead girls. A man who organized *prostitution* at the same time as being a teacher, picking up vulnerable, homeless girls and tempting them into a life of abuse. The police would love to know about it, I was sure.

Did it make him a killer, though? I remembered the night before, the rasping sounds of someone's breathing behind me and the strong hands that grabbed my shoulders and pushed me headlong towards the river. It was something else I would have to tell Heather about.

I rang the bell and waited for a few minutes for her voice on the intercom. I said my name and without a word a sharp buzz sounded and the outside door of her block opened. She was waiting for me at her front door, wearing jeans and a T-shirt, looking casual.

"Patsy," she smiled. "This is a surprise."

I mumbled some polite stuff and walked into her flat with her. She was wearing a strong perfume and there was the sound of low jazzy music. I could also see an unopened bottle of wine and two glasses on the side.

"You're expecting someone?" I said.

"A friend. But he's not due for an hour or so. Come in. I'll make a coffee. It's nice to see you."

"It's not really a social call, Heather. I think I've found an important lead in the river Lea murders."

"Oh?" she said and gave me a long quizzical look. "I've got this special Turkish coffee. You start talking while I put the kettle on."

I told her everything, the interviews I'd done, the visits I'd made, the meeting with Tanya. Finally, the revelation about Mike Crosby.

I'd known Heather since I started working for my uncle Tony about eighteen months before. She'd been a colleague of his in the local CID. She'd been promoted rapidly above the men in the office because she was good at her job. My uncle didn't like her much, but I did. She was sharp and quick and not afraid to criticize me if she thought I was wrong. She also trusted me and went out of her way to help me when I needed it.

"Mike Crosby! The second girl's teacher!" she said. The coffee was in a cafetière and she pushed the plunger down slowly and thoughtfully.

"There's the link," I said, excitedly. "There's no one in the case who had any real association with both the girls. This man has and he's lied about it, denied it."

"With good reason. A school teacher, running a flat with teenage prostitutes. It's almost unbelievable. How did he get away with it?"

She poured the coffee into tiny cups with saucers. It had the consistency of crude oil but I took a sip anyway.

"It's a real breakthrough," she said, sipping hers and licking her lips after each mouthful, "I'm on duty early in the morning and I'll have the guy brought in for questioning. You've done well, Patsy.

This could be the opening that we need."

"Thing is," I said playing with the tiny cup, "I'm wondering if it wouldn't be better to get moving more quickly. Maybe pull him in tonight."

"But why? It's been over a year now. He's not going anywhere and he has no idea that you saw him at the house in Hammersmith. Why rush it?"

There was no other way except to blurt out the truth. "Because I think he tried to kill me last night."

"What?" she smiled and then said, "What?" again, as though she hadn't heard me.

"Someone tried to drown me last night. Down at the river Lea."

She stopped, pushed her cup aside and said, "Oh, Patsy, why didn't you tell me straight away? Honestly, when are you going to learn?"

"I'm here now," I said, stiffly. The last thing I needed was a telling off.

It was nine o'clock when I turned the corner and walked into my own street. Even though it was dark I could see, further up, Billy's car parked on the other side. The lights were off but I could see him sitting in the driver's seat. As I got closer I could hear the muted sound of music. I tapped on the window and he wound it down, leaning across to lower the sound.

"Hi," I said, mildly embarrassed, not quite knowing what to say after the row. On the passenger's seat I could see my rucksack.

"I got your message. I tried to call but you've been out all day."

"I've been working," I said. "Why are you sitting out here?"

"Your mum's out. I thought I'd hang around a while and see if you came back."

He put his hand out and rubbed my arm, affectionately.

It was only a small gesture but it made me go weak in the legs. I put my hand in the window and pushed my fingers into his hair. Then I bent over and kissed him hard, feeling the *whoosh* of a motorcycle pass behind me.

"This is too dangerous," he laughed when I stopped. "You could get yourself killed doing it."

I watched the tail light of the bike disappear up the street.

"I've got some stuff to tell you," I said. "Let's go for a burger."

We went to McDonald's Drive Thru. All the way there I told him about what had happened the previous evening. He was quiet at first saying things like, "What?... Did you see anyone? ... Which bit of the river exactly? ... Under the bridge? ... Have you still got the envelope and the ribbon? ... How did they get you out? ... Oh, Patsy, you could have drowned."

Then he wanted me to tell it to him over again. Right from the beginning, the letter under the door of the office, the walk from the dark car park along the river. "Who did you pass? ... Exactly what time was it? ... What about the people working in the rowing school?"

We edged forward in the queue for our food and his voice rose an octave.

"Did no one see anything? ... What about the guys in the mobile café? ... Or the people who used the pub? ... What did the police say?

"Oh, Patsy, you could have been killed."

We ordered a couple of burgers, fries and drinks. Inside the brightly lit windows I could see the girl with the headset relaying the orders for the food to the backstage kids who were sweating around the griddles. She was blonde and speaking softly and she had one finger lightly on her microphone. Her eyes were distant, looking far away into the dark night and I had this sudden picture of her as a singer on a stage adjusting her headset.

"Here's your order." Her voice came like the first notes of a song. "Enjoy your meal!"

I held the food as Billy edged the car forward.

"Oh, Patsy, I could have been helping your mum to organize your funeral tonight."

I refused to speak and sunk down into the passenger's seat, the heat from the food warming up my lap.

I knew that. How could he think I didn't know that?

# 16

# The Photograph

I could hardly sleep with excitement.

Heather rang me and said that they were bringing Mike Crosby in for questioning. I'd wanted to be there but she'd said that was impossible. I had to leave it to the police. She was going to ring me first thing in the morning and tell me what had happened. I felt a bit like the kid who has had his football taken from him and been told to go home while the other kids played with it.

She also told me that they were arranging for a diver to go to the river Lea and retrieve the envelope and the pink ribbon that I'd lost. I'd mentioned my mobile phone then. I knew it would probably never work again but for some reason I still wanted it back.

Billy stayed with me until my mum and Gerry got home. I made him promise not to say anything to my mum about my dip in the river. We stood on the doorstep for a few minutes like young kids at the end of a date. He kept pushing his face into my hair and shaking his head. As he left he told me not to worry about anything and that we'd talk about *that other thing* later. I suspected he meant the new job and the year in Africa. My spirits took a dip just remembering it.

I lay in the dark for ages listening to the sounds from the TV downstairs and the water running in the bathroom, followed by the toilet flushing. I kept moving around, lying on my back with my arms crossed over in front of me, then turning on my side with my knees up high touching my elbows. A couple of times I lay up on one elbow looking at the clock and listening to the pipes gurgling as the central heating boiler came to a weary stop and packed up for the night.

Had Mike Crosby been the person who had killed the two girls? It seemed unlikely but the new evidence was pointing a big arrow in his direction. I let a story piece itself together in my head. Mike Crosby had a sideline to being a sixth-form college teacher: a "business" where he looked after homeless teenage girls in return for their cooperation with his older men friends. At first Susan Yorke had turned him down, laughed at him, pinched his box of chocolates and took herself and Tanya away from the house in Hammersmith. But then after Christmas, when she was down on her luck, word had it that she'd gone back there. How long she had stayed "working" for Mike Crosby, no one knew. Could it have been until a couple of weeks before Valentine's Day when she'd got fed up, perhaps discovered that this man who used her services in the most uncaring way was also a schoolteacher? An overheard phone call? A bit of gossip from other girls?

She had threatened to expose him. He had bided his time, found out that she'd been hanging around with some kids down at the river Lea. There'd been a lot of alcohol and parties and perhaps Mike Crosby had devised a way to get rid of the troublesome girl who knew his secret and could ruin him. Make it look like a dare that had gone wrong.

Jennifer Ryan had been his student and had spent a couple of days working at St Michael's, decorating a room. Had she stumbled on the secret of the house at Hammersmith? Or had she found out some other way?

The link was there somewhere, I was sure. It was the details that were hard to fit in. After a long time trying I must have fallen into a sleep.

When I awoke it was 03:05.

I turned over, plumping up the pillow with my fists, and wondered if they'd arrested him yet. I lay and imagined what might have happened. They'd gone to his house where his young wife lived. Maybe Heather had gone with another officer. They'd knocked on the door and he'd answered it. Or his wife had answered it and looked surprised. She'd called out his name. "Mike, there's a couple of police officers and they say they want to talk to you." Possibly she'd turned to Heather and complained, "Couldn't you people have waited until the morning? I've got children asleep upstairs."

Heather would have kept calm, smiling and waiting for Mike Crosby to come to the door. "Do you mind if we talk to you in private, sir?" she would have said.

If only I had been there. It hadn't been possible, though. A private detective isn't ever part of the main action. We just wander up and down the sidelines shouting directions and advice at the real players, the police. Mostly they ignore us; occasionally they're forced into talking our advice.

I must have fallen asleep sometimes during the football game and when I woke up it was 05:38. I lay there for a few minutes, the events of the previous day going through my head. My eyelids, usually glued together for the first fifteen or so minutes every morning, had sprung open and I was completely wide awake. I got out of bed and shuffled around finding my dressing gown and slippers. I didn't imagine that Heather would ring me much before seven, so I decided to get up and make myself something, even though I didn't feel much like eating.

The smell of toast awakened my appetite and I got the peanut butter and jam out. I made a cup of tea and sat down at the kitchen table, gazing idly at the window which looked on to the back garden. It was mostly dark but there was a hint of daybreak in the charcoal sky. Would Mike Crosby be in custody? I heard a noise from somewhere and thought that perhaps my mum or Gerry had woken up.

For some reason, Tanya came into my head. Standing by the side of Alice she'd looked like a little girl, her dog at her heels, like a toy that she'd been given. I thought of her ginger hair and freckles, her face like that of a doll. Was there nobody who cared for her? Who wondered where she might have gone? Maybe there was a bedroom somewhere, with soft toys and books and a pink nightie stuffed inside a heart-shaped case. Maybe there was a parent or brother who thought about her every day and wondered what she was doing.

I thought of my own mum and what it might be like if I suddenly went away and never saw her again. A stupid lump formed in my throat and the job in Africa came into my mind. It wasn't the same thing at all, I knew that, but it was still thousands of miles away from where I wanted to be.

Then the phone rang and I was jolted out of my reverie. I took giant steps out along the hallway so that the ringing wouldn't wake anyone else up and noticed that the mail had been delivered and a letter lay, face down, on the mat. I picked the receiver up and found myself whispering.

"It's Heather, Patsy. I hope I haven't woken your family up, only I'm about to go on to a meeting and I thought you'd want to know what happened."

"Yes?" I said.

"Honestly, Patsy, he's as cool as a cucumber. Didn't bat an eyelid when we mentioned the house in Hammersmith. He just asked for a phone call and rang a solicitor. It was a number that he knew off by heart. An hour later this City type comes along, pin-striped suit, white shirt, grey tie, all of this in the middle of the night."

"Were you able to charge him with anything? Did you ask about Susan Yorke?"

"I'm coming to that. He had this talk with his solicitor. Then we interviewed him. His solicitor just kept saying, 'My client has no comment to make.' When we finally get to asking him about the murders, he did have a comment, or at least his solicitor, who sat there like a pin-striped ventriloquist's dummy, gave us two alibis for the nights in question. On Valentine's night Crosby was with his wife at a local pub party. There are at least a dozen people that will say he was there. A month later, and here's the really concrete alibi, he was in hospital having some treatment for kidney stones."

"What about the house?" I said, rocked with disappointment.

"My officers went there last night. It's managed by a renting agency. There's six flats and only four of them are occupied at the moment. They all seem like bona fide tenants. Crosby made no comment. The thing is, Patsy, we'll probably find out that his name's not actually on any lease or rent book. These people are too clever for that. Then all we'll have is the girl's word against his."

Tanya's word against Mike Crosby's.

"What about my word?" I said. "I saw him pull up outside the house in his car?"

"He'll say it was coincidence. He'll say, if his solicitor ever allows him to speak, that he'd lost his way around London and was stopping to ask someone."

"Oh."

Every word Heather spoke seemed to be a door closing against me. I'd found a link but it wasn't the neat solution that I'd wanted. My eye wandered to the letter that was lying face down on the mat and I remembered that it was Sunday. The day when there was no post.

"Don't get downhearted, Patsy. We'll have to let Crosby go in a couple of hours but we've got our eye on him and our officers over in West London will be looking into the Hammersmith link. One thing is clear, though. He didn't kill the girls. His alibis are too strong."

I put the phone down and huffed. I felt like I'd just climbed to the top of a hill, only to find that there was another one behind. I could hear the sounds of movement from upstairs and I slouched across the hall to pick up the letter.

"Patsy, is that you on the phone?" It was my mum's voice.

"Yes," I said, turning the envelope over in my hand.

There was no address, just the words PATSY KELLY printed on the front. I turned it over a couple of times, looking at it stupidly. For a microsecond I had this light-headed feeling, this mild dizziness, so I sat down on the bottom stair and looked closely at the envelope for a few moments before I pushed my finger into the corner and opened it.

"Put the kettle on, will you, Patsy? I'll be down in a minute." My mum's voice came from upstairs.

Inside there were several bits of something, like a tiny jigsaw. I poured the pieces out on to the stairs and saw fragments of a black and white photograph of myself. A bad feeling was worming around inside my stomach and I picked up the pieces one by one as though they were shards of an expensive broken vase. It was a recent shot, taken the day before, I was sure. I recognized the outside of St Michael's hostel and myself walking along. I was either on my way there or walking out just ahead of Tanya.

Someone had taken a photograph of me and cut it up in pieces. I looked back at the envelope and saw that inside there was a small slip of white paper and a single ringlet of pink ribbon. I pulled them out and saw, in the neatest print, the words, KEEP OUT, PATSY, OR YOU'RE NEXT.

My mum's footsteps came towards the top of the stairs and I shoved everything back into the envelope.

"Who was that on the phone at this time?" she said, stretching her arms up to the ceiling.

"Just something about the case," I said, slipping the envelope inside my dressing gown.

So Mike Crosby, whatever else he had done, wasn't responsible for the deaths of the two girls. Someone else had killed them. Whoever it was had tried to frighten me off once already and didn't seem to be about to give up.

# 17

# Searching for Links

Billy picked me up about eight and we drove to the police station. I left the envelope with the fragmented photograph and a note to Heather explaining what had happened. I told her I'd be back about lunchtime.

We went straight to St Michael's and picked up Tanya. I had an idea that another chat with her might give me some more information. I was clutching at straws, really. Somebody was threatening me, perhaps watching me, and I didn't have any idea who it might be. It was important to keep busy, that's what I told myself.

Tanya struggled out the door of the hostel looking grumpy. Her eyes were screwed up as though she'd been hibernating for months. When she saw that I had Billy with me she hesitated.

"Who's he? I told Alice I don't like getting involved with strangers."

"He's a good mate," I said. "I just want you to come with us, talk to us about you and Susan during those weeks before you fell out at Christmas."

"I told you everything I knew already. What happened about Mickey and the house in Hammersmith?"

"I'll tell you as we go along," I said. "Please. I'll buy you a nice breakfast."

She shrugged her shoulders and got into the back seat of the car. Tiggy immediately followed her on to the seat.

"Does that dog have to sit on my upholstery?" Billy said, looking aghast.

"If he don't come, I don't come," Tanya said, sulkily.

I raised my eyebrows to Billy, and he turned and started the engine.

The river Lea was the busiest I had ever seen it. Within a couple of minutes half a dozen small rowing boats passed us, the rowers' arms moving in perfect synchrony, as though they were part of some carefully crafted display. One of the long barges was gliding slowly towards us, a man sitting on the top, legs crossed, reading a newspaper. There were some kids playing over on the other bank and a couple of people walking their dogs.

It was a cold, bright day and the sun was speckled

on the water.

We stood by *Aquarius Foods* and ate bacon rolls with polystyrene cups of hot tea. Tanya finished hers first and then looked hungrily at the hotplate and then at Ian Payne as he was cracking an egg for another man who was waiting.

"You want something else, Tanya?" Billy said.

Tanya shrugged in a moody way and I nudged Billy, nodding my head. He bought her a fried egg sandwich.

"You recovered from the other night?" Alan Payne said, walking round the front of the stall and throwing some cut-up bread to the nearby ducks.

"Just about," I said, grimacing. "I meant to ask you if you'd had any luck with my card."

He gave me a puzzled look.

"Remember you said you might ask some of the regular café users about the two girls who were murdered here last year?"

"Oh, that!" he said, breaking into a laugh. "Indeed I did. I mentioned it to a couple of guys. No one has said anything. I'll keep asking, though. You never know!"

"Thanks, I'm really grateful."

"Have you been here long?" Billy said.

"About nine months or so. It's a good spot. It was slow at first but business has been picking up."

I looked over at Tanya. She was kneeling down, feeding the last bit of her egg sandwich to Tiggy.

Would it be a good idea, I wondered, to introduce her to Kerry Yorke? What if they spent a bit of time together? Tanya had a lot of stuff that she could tell Kerry about Susan's last months.

"I've often wondered about these small businesses," Billy carried on talking. "You see them dotted about and wonder whether they really make any money."

"A living. They make a living. We don't want a lot though, me and Ian. We're just happy getting by. Aren't we, Ian?"

Ian Payne looked up and grunted. Not the greatest conversationalist, I thought.

"What we doing?" Tanya said, rubbing her arms. She was getting bored.

"We're just going to walk up the river a bit," I said, "then we've got to go to the police station."

"It better not take too long. I've got stuff to do and people to see!" she said, marching off along the path. I smiled at her words.

"Billy!" I said and pointed in the direction that she was going.

"Nice talking to you," I could hear Billy saying as I followed Tanya along the river bank.

The three of us sat on the Waterside bench, across from the rowing club. There were a number of people milling about, lifting boats and getting ready to launch them on to the river. In front of us a family of ducks made their way along, the mother out front, avoiding the litter and debris that was bobbing up and down.

Tanya went over all the things she'd told me the day before. Billy prompted her a bit, hoping to jog her memory further, but to no avail. After a while, she got a bit sniffy and said that she was cold and needed some lunch. She didn't move, though. She seemed quite comfortable there in the middle of us, her dog at her feet. I suspected that she didn't really have stuff to do or people to see.

From time to time, I found myself distractedly looking up towards the concrete bridge where someone had hidden, waiting for me to pass so that they could push me in. Just passing the spot had made me freeze, my fingers stiffening with tension. I'd forced myself on, though. I'd made a mistake the other night but I couldn't let it stop me from following up the case. The photograph was another worry. I'd given it to the police for forensic examination and I vowed to have someone, probably Billy, with me at all times during the next few days. I was taking precautions but I really had to keep going. I remembered Kerry Yorke's words: "I'm depending on you, Patsy," and the photo she'd given me of a younger Susan, smiling toothily at the camera. Someone was responsible for her death and it wasn't right that they were going about their lives as though nothing had happened.

But it was odd, to start the case with no hope, to achieve something, to rattle a killer and turn up new information and to still find myself back at the beginning with nothing. It was like a game of

Monopoly; early hopes, false moves, *Go to jail, do not collect £200.*

"The truth is," I said, "we're back to square one."

"What?" said Tanya, who had clearly been on some other train of thought entirely.

"OK," Billy said, businesslike, "let's go back to square one. You said there was a missing link here. Let's look for a link between the two girls."

"That's what I've been doing."

"Yes, but you've been looking at places they went to or people they knew. Couldn't it be that somebody killed them just because of something superficial about them? Like they had the same birthmarks or both of them only had four fingers or something?"

"Susan didn't have four fingers," Tanya said, looking incredulous.

"I know that, but mightn't there be something obvious like that? Something that everyone's missed?"

I was doubtful but I got the files out of my ruck-sack and turned to the two neatly typed out pages that I had headed up with the girls' names.

"Here," I said, handing them to Billy.

"No," he said. "You look through them while I make some suggestions."

I sat back on the bench and felt Tanya lean against me.

"Hair?"

"Susan's was short and dyed red. Jennifer's was long and blonde."

"OK. Complexion, facial features, height, weight, stuff like that."

"Susan: light skin, brown eyes, five foot five, eight-and-a-half stone. Jennifer: light skin, blue eyes, five foot six, eight stone."

"OK," he said, thinking. Then he went on with his list: clothes size, shoe size, jewellery, make-up, perfume, deodorant, hair fastenings, handbag, dress labels.

"Dress labels?" Tanya said.

"They might have bought their clothes from the same shops?" Billy shrugged.

"Honestly, Patsy, is your mate completely thick? Susan didn't buy any clothes. She was homeless. She didn't have the money!"

"OK," Billy went on, undeterred. "Date of birth?"

"Susan was born on December twenty-ninth and Jennifer's birthday was January eighteenth. Not even the same month."

"Accent? Did they both speak with a different accent?"

"Hardly," I said. Billy was getting desperate and we were getting nowhere. I looked at my watch. It was almost lunchtime, the time I said I'd bring Tanya into the police station.

"Not the same months, but the same star sign," Tanya said.

"What?" Billy turned and looked at Tanya.

"They weren't born in the same months, Susie

155

and that other girl, but it is under the same star sign. Capricorn, see? December twenty-first to January nineteenth."

I nodded my head. She was right but I couldn't imagine what it might have to do with the case. I noticed, across the way, a small police van driving up the track through the rowing club. It stopped near the edge and a man in a wetsuit got out and started to talk to someone from the rowing club. It was the police divers. They were going to swim out to the spot where I'd gone in and purposely go under the thick water to look for the stuff I had dropped.

"Capricorn. That's what they've got in common," Tanya repeated, in a bored voice. "They were both born under the same star sign."

"I'll make a note of it," I said, writing the word *Capricorn* across the page. I stood up ready to go, my eyes avoiding the man in the wetsuit, my mind trying to ignore the picture of him going down into the muddy blackness.

"Let's get you to the police station," I said, starting to walk along.

"You'll wait with me, won't you?" Tanya said, linking her arm through mine.

"Course I will," I said and we walked up the river path, the three of us deep in thought, me and Billy on the outside and Tanya in the middle. Only the dog looked carefree, his tail wagging at everything that moved.

# 18

# Afshan Begum

We spent most of the afternoon at the police station. Tanya wouldn't let go of me and I found myself in all her interviews. She refused to give her full name in case her mum found out. No amount of persuasion by the pleasant plainclothes WPC would make any difference. About five-thirty we took her back to St Michael's hostel, bought her some fish and chips and said goodbye. I gave her my home phone number and asked her to ring me. She nodded but looked deflated. The excitement of the day had disappeared and now she was back into her routine.

I still had it in the back of my mind to introduce her to Kerry Yorke. Another part of me cautioned against it. Tanya would be able to tell Kerry about

Susan's last months, about her wish to go back home, but she would also be able to tell her about the house in Hammersmith and the fact that Susan had spent some time there before she died.

During the afternoon I'd spent some serious time with Heather Warren, who had outlined some simple security precautions I was to take.

"My thoughts are that this man is simply trying to scare you off, Patsy, but I think we have to be careful all the same. I'm going to ask the local patrol car and bobby to keep an eye on your house at regular intervals; as well as that, I want you to phone into the police station with a password four times a day. That way I can be sure that you're all right."

"You won't tell my mum or my uncle about any of this?" I said.

"You'll have to tell Tony sometime. You're meant to be working together, after all."

"I know," I said. "I'll tell him first thing tomorrow when I'm back at work."

"OK, but make sure you don't forget to ring in to us."

She said it sharply as though there might be dire consequences if I didn't. I was a smidgen irked, but then I found myself relaxing and not feeling so uncomfortable when I thought about my photo sitting in pieces in a police file.

"What's going to happen to Mike Crosby?"

"Nothing at the moment. Vice Squad officers in

Hammersmith are looking for some evidence against him. It may well be that he gets away with it."

"But you've got Tanya's statement now!"

"Patsy, look at the kind of witness Tanya would make. A homeless kid up against sharp, expensive barristers. Up against an established school teacher and family man. No, we need something else."

"It's not right," I said.

"You get your mind off Mike Crosby and back on to your own security. Do you hear me? This is deadly serious."

She opened her office door and let me out, her eyes darting about, her mind already on something else.

The next morning I stayed at home. About eleven I rang the office and spoke to my uncle Tony, who had just got back from his conference and was bubbling with it. After a few murmurs of interest I managed to get him to stay quiet long enough to tell him what had happened over the weekend. Not all of it, just the stuff he needed to know. I also told him that I intended to work from home for the next few days. He didn't seem bothered. He was probably glad to have the office to himself for a while. I told him to pass on any phone calls that sounded important. Then I hung up.

The truth was I felt like leaving it alone for a

while. Being pushed into the river had upset me more than I'd admitted and every now and then I got this cringing feeling in my stomach and a moment's total panic so that I had to stop what I was doing and take deep breaths.

In the afternoon I went round to Billy's and watched two videos in a row and had a giant bag of Maltesers all to myself. Billy sat on the settee with his hand in my hair and from time to time he gave me a hug.

We drove back to my house about six. Billy was chatting amiably about this and that and I realized then that in the previous couple of days he hadn't mentioned his new job or his future plans. He was avoiding the subject and so was I. No doubt it would come up later.

As I put the key in the door my mum opened it.

"There's someone here to see you," she said. "She rang four times this afternoon and sounded almost tearful on the last call so I told her to come round."

"Who?" I said, looking puzzled.

"Afshan, her name is. She's been sitting as quiet as a mouse in the living room."

We went in and an Asian girl immediately stood up, looking awkward and out of place. She was wearing jeans and a zip-up jacket. Her hair was very long, heavy and straight near the roots but curly at the ends as if she'd had a perm at some time. She had a lot of jewellery on, earrings, chains, rings and bracelets.

"Hi, I'm Patsy," I said, smiling. Afshan Begum. The name was unfamiliar and yet *Afshan* had a ring to it.

"What can I do for you?"

She looked at me and then at Billy and then back to me. She wasn't comfortable, I could sense.

"Billy, any chance of a cup of tea?" I said.

"Sure," he said. "Sugar? Milk?" he asked Afshan.

When he went I sat down and said, in a gentle voice, "What did you want to see me about?"

"I was a friend of Jenny Ryan's. We went to school together. St Mary's, a girls-only school in Bethnal Green."

"But I didn't meet you at the college?"

"No, I don't go there. My father. He didn't want me to go to a mixed college. He's pretty strict, doesn't want me mixing with boys."

"How did you get my number?"

"Lesley, at the college? Black girl you saw?"

I nodded my head.

"She gave me your card. I got through to the office number and a man gave me this number."

"And you've got something you want to tell me?"

"I should have gone to the police, last year, when she was killed but I didn't dare." Her voice was breaking and I noticed that her hand was trembling.

"Why don't you tell me about it?"

161

"See, Jenny and me, we stayed friends even though she went to the college. I mean, she had her mates there but she still saw me, when I could get out, that is. Trouble is my father, he just didn't want me going to the college or out at night. We had big rows but in the end it wasn't worth upsetting the family. He paid for me to go on a private secretarial course and I pretended the hours were longer than they actually were so that I could get out with Jenny. I also told him there were night classes."

"And he didn't find out?"

"No. Me and Jenny spent a bit of time together. Course she was going out with that idiot Steve but she was fed up with him."

I could hear the clinking of dishes from the other room and my mum's voice chatting to Billy. Afshan was playing with her rings, building up to something. Then I remembered where I'd heard her name before. *Affie.* Steven White had said that the last time he'd seen Jennifer alive was when she'd been talking to Affie outside the college.

"Jenny fell for this older, married guy. She didn't tell anyone else about it but me. She said she couldn't trust any of the college kids. That's why she spent so much time with me. I met him a couple of times at these parties in this flat in Hammersmith."

"Hammersmith?" I said, perking up.

"I had to lie like hell to get out. I told my dad that Jenny's mum was ill and that I was staying there to help her out. He allowed me to stay three times and we went to these parties over at Hammersmith. She told her mum she was staying with me. We took a real chance but nobody found out."

"What was his name, this man? What did he look like?"

I had Mike Crosby in mind. The personal tutor, the smooth operator in the BMW. I was almost crossing my fingers in the hope that it was him.

"She fell in love with him but he was married and had little babies. There was no chance he was ever going to leave his wife for her. I knew that. She just couldn't see it. In the end, in those last days before she was killed, I hardly saw her. Truth is we had a bit of a row. I stopped ringing her. She stopped ringing me. Next thing I heard she was dead."

"Who was the man, Afshan?" I said, hearing Billy coming in the door behind me.

"His name was Peter Lee. He was the warden of that place, that hostel where she did some decorating. He was good-looking but I told her he would never 'ave left his wife."

I took my tea like an automaton. Peter Lee had had an affair with Jennifer Ryan. The man who ran the hostel, who looked after the young, vulnerable homeless, had had an affair with a college girl. Why had no one seen that?

"Why didn't you go to the police? Didn't you know how important that information might have been?"

"I was in shock. When she was killed I just froze. My parents were upset, everyone was upset, she was one of my best friends! I almost went to the police. Three, four times I almost got as far as the station but it would 'ave meant admitting to my dad what I'd been doing, that I'd been lying to him. You don't know what that would 'ave meant for my family."

"But she was murdered."

"But so was the other girl and I thought, how can it have anything to do with what Jenny was doing or who she was seeing?"

"Peter Lee knew her, though. He knew her and he knew Jenny."

"But you see," she was moving round in her chair with agitation, "the first party we went to in the house in Hammersmith was on Valentine's night. That was when Jenny and him got it together."

"Valentine's night," Billy said, giving me a knowing look.

"That's it. That was the night the first girl was killed. See what I'm saying. Peter Lee couldn't 'ave killed her because he was there with us. So when Jenny died I thought that it couldn't 'ave had anything to do with him. Not if both girls were killed by the same person. See what I mean?"

I did see what she meant.

"That's sort of why I didn't come forward. Not exactly. The reason I didn't come forward was because I knew my father would go up the wall if he found out that I'd lied to him. The fact that I was sure Peter Lee never killed Jenny, that was my excuse."

I felt like someone had just handed me some sweets with one hand and then a couple of seconds later taken them away with the other. Peter Lee, who Alice said had gone through a messy divorce. Peter Lee who had links with Mike Crosby and the house in Hammersmith. Even if neither of them was the killer, it was a pretty poor show when two people who were supposed to be in charge of young people couldn't be trusted. I could hear Billy talking to Afshan, asking her where she lived and what she worked at.

It was all information I could pass on to Heather. It would help the Mike Crosby investigation – maybe Peter Lee had some information that would tie him more tightly to the house in Hammersmith and the accusation of prostitution.

But it didn't throw any light on the murder of the two girls. I drank the rest of my tea and wondered if we were any nearer to finding the person responsible than we had been at the beginning.

I rang Heather Warren and told her about the latest developments. She spoke to Afshan briefly, assuring her of confidentiality. I could hear Afshan agreeing to go into the police station the next day.

"She says my dad will never need to know," Afshan said, exhaling a great sigh. Her face broke into a smile and her body seemed to loosen up as she sat down and finished what was by then a cold cup of tea.

Billy and I gave her a lift home and all the way there she talked about Jennifer Ryan.

"Me and Jenny had lots in common. That's why I was so upset when my dad wouldn't let me go to the college. She wasn't as close to any of her other mates as she'd been to me. We were born in the same hospital, you know, went to the same primary and secondary school. We even had the same star sign. We were both Capricorns."

"Capricorns," I said, thinking of the obscure link between Jennifer and Susan.

"Yes. She was really into that stuff. She had books on it and always read her stars."

"I never read my stars," I said, thinking that it might be a good time to start.

"Course Jenny was popular at college and she never had any trouble getting off with boys. It wasn't unusual for her to have a couple going at once. She was seeing someone else when she met Steve White. Course she thought that she was in love with Peter Lee. But that was just because he was older and married. Because he belonged to someone else, she wanted him. She even tried making him jealous with some kid she picked up off the street. She told me that this kid was always willing to take her anywhere. He had a job driving and delivering stuff, so she'd get him to take her to the hostel, drop her off right in front so that Peter Lee could see she had another boyfriend."

"So, on top of the married man she had another lad in tow?" I said.

"I never met him, just somebody she used for a while and then dumped."

She didn't sound like a nice person, this Jennifer Ryan. Not nice at all.

We dropped Afshan off at the end of her street and drove back in silence. I thought over the last few days and tried to pull together what had been gained. Not much, when it came down to it. I had a lover for Jennifer who had a watertight alibi on the night of the first murder. I had another boyfriend who used to drive her around. And I had two murdered girls who were both born under the same star sign, Capricorn.

It was a Chinese puzzle and I was so absorbed in it that I didn't notice Billy pull up outside my house.

"I can't come round tomorrow," he said. "There's a training day I said I'd go on."

I shrugged my shoulders.

"It's OK. Maybe I'll go and see Kerry Yorke. Maybe I'll tell her I've done as much as I can."

Billy didn't speak. I thought he might say something about the new job but he didn't and I was glad.

"I'll see you when I see you," I said, leant over and kissed him on the lips and then got out of the car.

# 19

# The Van

When I woke up the next morning I had this major attack of inertia. I lay there in the grey of my bedroom and listened to the radio playing quietly. The time on the clock was 07:15. I'd spent just over a week on the case. I'd turned up two new witnesses. I'd found a couple of unsavoury links between the professionals who were supposed to look after young people and a seedy underworld. Oh, yeah, I'd received hate mail and been pushed into the river and left to die.

But I'd found nothing yet that explained how Kerry Yorke's daughter had come to be a murder victim.

What was I supposed to do? Continue digging? Or go and see Kerry and tell her that I'd done all I could? I dragged myself out of bed and pulled on some jeans and a sweatshirt. At seven-thirty, I needed to phone the police station and check in. Otherwise Heather would have a fleet of police cars looking for me.

The whole thing was tiresome. I stretched my arms up to the ceiling and let myself flop back on the bed. There was a quiet knock on the door and my mum's head appeared.

"I brought you a cup of tea," she said.

"Oh," I said, and sat up.

"Are you all right?" she said, sitting down on the bed next to me.

"Yes." I took the mug of tea and blew gently at the steam that was billowing out of it.

"I'm off to work in a minute but Gerry's staying around today, working on his dissertation. It won't bother you, if he's here in the house, I mean?"

"No," I said. It was the least of my worries.

"Will you be going into work at all?"

"Maybe. I'm not sure."

"Right. I appreciate the effort you've made, Patsy. I know it can't be easy, having someone else around after years of living on our own."

"I've hardly noticed him," I said. It was the truth. I'd been so preoccupied with the case that I probably wouldn't have noticed if we'd had the local football team staying. I was also grateful that he'd been around to pick me up from the river Lea and, it seemed, had kept his word and not said anything about it.

My mum got up and walked across to the window and pulled the curtains back. I found myself looking at my rucksack in the corner. Inside it was the dead mobile phone. I'd need to take it back to the shop and see about a replacement.

"The police are all over the place these days," she said. "There was a patrol car parked outside last night for about fifteen minutes and this morning, when I was out for my run, I noticed another one!"

"Maybe there's been a burglary," I said, casually. "Um…"

She left a few moments later, giving me a kiss on the cheek and ruffling my hair. It was an unusual show of affection and I put it down to her gratitude. I could afford to be generous over Gerry. It wasn't as though he was going to stay for ever.

I made a plan. I would go to the mobile phone shop and see about replacing the phone. Then I would definitely go and see Kerry Yorke. I'd leave it up to her to decide whether I should continue with the case or not.

I went downstairs and made my phone call to the police station, giving the code word so that they knew it was really me. The next call I had to make was at two-thirty. Then I had some breakfast.

Before going out I decided to have a general tidy up. It was something I liked to do whenever I was under stress. Some people call it a displacement activity. That's when you do one thing to put off doing something else. I just enjoyed taking my mind off things and doing something completely different.

I got my clothes out of the wardrobe and laid them all flat out on the bed. I pulled out a couple of skirts that hadn't seen the light of day for years and threw them to a spot by the door. Then I looked at my shoes, two pairs of trainers, two pairs of DMs and one pair of what my mum called *ladylike shoes*. She'd bought them for me when I'd started working for my uncle eighteen months before. I turned them over. The soles were almost unmarked. I went to throw them on the pile of unwanted stuff but then changed my mind. My mum would notice if they weren't there.

I got my hats down from the top of my wardrobe. I dusted the boxes and tried a few on that I hadn't worn for a while. Then I found a dark blue velvet one that had a narrow brim. I'd had it for years, I was sure. I put it on my head and was immediately pleased, so I left it on my dressing-table to wear.

After I'd put everything back I sat down at the mirror and wondered whether to put some make-up on. Since my swim in the river I hadn't bothered much with the way I looked. As well as that there'd been the row with Billy and the fact that I hadn't really got anywhere with the case. I needed to pep myself up, to get myself going again. The word *makeover* came into my head and I felt a buzz of interest inside.

Don't get me wrong, I'm not obsessed with the way I look. I don't concern myself with trying to look *beautiful*, whatever that is. I just want to look interesting. I just want people to look at me and wonder where I got my scarf or my beads or why I wore those boots with that skirt. Of course I want people to notice me, I'd be a liar if I said I didn't. But I don't spend my time wishing I looked like the supermodels or film stars. I just wanted to look like myself but a bit *different*.

I picked up my rucksack and felt deep inside it for my make-up bag. It was full of stuff, though, and I ended up pulling out an address book, my glasses case, this small mock-zebra purse I've got and three half-used packets of tissues. I took the rucksack over to my bed and tipped it up, opening all the flaps and pockets. It was high time I gave it a clear out, as well as my room.

There was a lot of junk, mostly print-outs from the computer, a lot of it to do with the river Lea murders. I made a pile, flattening out crumpled sheets of paper. There was my notebook, an A-Z of London, two small plastic brushes, my make-up bag and an empty plastic triangle that had once held a sandwich. There were several leaflets I had picked up and a very old copy of *The Big Issue* that must have been there for weeks and weeks.

My rucksack was like the Tardis from *Doctor Who*, bigger on the inside. I started to clear away the rubbish and replace the stuff I needed in the canvas bag. I took the magazine and leaflets and empty sandwich packet and was about to chuck them into the bin when I noticed something. At least, my eye seemed drawn to the plastic triangle and the label that was on the front of it. *Capricorn Sandwiches. Free Delivery.* I threw the rest of the stuff in the bin and sat back to look at it. *Capricorn.* The star sign that Susan and Jennifer had been born under. The one similarity between them.

I thought back to when I'd got the sandwich and, as I remembered, little lights seemed to go on inside my head. I'd bought the sandwich while waiting to see the Singing Dentist. The young man had come in and I'd been sitting waiting and felt the pangs of hunger. He'd been pleasant, friendly, had laughed with me about the Singing Dentist. As I'd left I'd seen him loading his empty tray into the back of his van. Closing my eyes, I thought back. The words on the van had said *Capricorn Sandwiches. Free Delivery.*

He'd been driving a van. I remembered Roger Dawkins then, the barge owner, talking about the van that Susan Yorke had got out of. I grabbed my pad off the bed and flicked through the pages until I got to the notes I'd made. *Company van, dark colour, words on the side to do with plants or farming.* Corn.

*Capricorn*. The van that had dropped Susan off had belonged to the sandwich company.

Afshan Begum had said that Jennifer Ryan had picked up someone who was happy to drive her around. A young man who had a job "driving and delivering stuff". The kind of job that needed a van. A company van. Perhaps the same van that had dropped Susan Yorke off. Then I remembered something the dentist had said. Susan's appointment had been at twelve-fifteen and Jennifer's three appointments were all in the lunch hour. All the appointments would have placed the girls there when the sandwich van came.

I got up and walked around my bedroom. It was a link but an odd one. There were too many *ifs* and *buts*. I needed to try it out on someone. Billy wasn't due to come round for a while and I didn't want to ring Heather in case the whole idea was just too slight, too silly.

Gerry was in the back sitting-room, his books and files spread out on the table. There was an empty cup and a plate with crumbs on it by his side.

"Gerry, hear me out," I said excitedly. "I want to suggest a set of events to you and see what you think."

"Fire away," he said, smiling easily, his hands loosely clasped across his big stomach.

"OK. You have to go to the dentist. Your appointment is at lunchtime and you're sitting, in the waiting room, reading magazines or whatever."

"I haven't been to the dentist's for years," Gerry said, taking his spectacles off and cleaning them with the end of his shirt.

"Never mind that. Just pretend. Oh, I forgot to say, you're a Capricorn. That's your birth sign."

"I'm a Taurus, me, the bull. It fits, doesn't it? Even though I think it's all a load of rubbish."

"Oh please, Gerry, concentrate. You're a Capricorn and this guy comes into the waiting room with a tray full of sandwiches to sell. Across his hat is the name of the company."

"Yes?" Gerry says, expectantly.

"It's called *Capricorn Sandwiches*. What would you do, what would you say?"

I waited while he looked at me.

"I'd probably see if he had a roast beef and mustard on granary."

"No!" I said, not sure if he was joking or not.

"If you mean would I mention the fact that the name of his company was the same as my birth sign…"

"Yes?"

"I don't know. Probably not."

"But if you were a young girl who thought stuff like that was important, stuff to do with the stars. Might you not comment on it? Say, 'That's a coincidence, I'm a Capricorn!'"

He sat looking at me and I could see that it wasn't fitting neatly.

"Why don't you ask the guy, the one who sold the sandwiches?" he said.

"I intend to," I said, and took my notebook out to the phone in the hall.

I dialled the dentist's number and tapped my fingers on the table while it rang. I looked in my book for the name of the receptionist and when she answered I spoke in my most polite voice.

"Is that Sue Wright?" I said, remembering her dark hair and blood-red lipstick.

"Yes."

"My name is Patsy Kelly and I came in to see you and Mr Silver a few days ago, you may remember. I was looking into the deaths of Susan Yorke and Jennifer Ryan."

"I do remember you, dear. You left me your little card. I've got it here by the computer. I'm afraid I haven't remembered anything else. It seems such a long time ago."

"I know," I said. "Thing is, I'm interested in the sandwich delivery company that came the day I was there, *Capricorn Sandwiches*. Were they the ones who delivered last year, when Susan and Jennifer came to the surgery?"

"Yes, I should think so, dear. They've been coming here for years. Since the bakery on the corner closed down."

"You don't happen to have the name of the boy who delivers the sandwiches?"

"Terry. You mean Terry the blond lad, or John, the dark lad?"

"There's two of them?"

"At the moment. I should think over the last year there've been about eight. It's not the sort of job kids stick at."

"No," I said. My fingers had stopped tapping, nothing was ever simple.

"Ring up the company, dear. They'll have a list of people who've worked for them," she said helpfully.

I thanked her and replaced the phone. The lad I had spoken to hadn't been working there at the time of the river Lea murders. It had been someone else. I went back into the living room and told Gerry.

"Ask them, the company." He said it stretching his arms up to the ceiling.

"They're not likely to give that sort of information over the phone. Not to me anyhow, someone they've never met and don't know anything about."

"You need to make up a good story. Here, let me try," Gerry said. "Got their number?"

I ran up the stairs and plucked the sandwich packet off the bed and took it back down to Gerry. He was standing at the phone in the hall and he punched in the numbers.

"Good morning," he said. "I'm calling from EastEnd Insurance Assessors. May I speak to the manager of *Capricorn Sandwiches*?"

There was a silence as Gerry nodded his head and

then seemed to wait for a minute. He put his hand over the receiver and mouthed something at me. I guessed they were putting him through.

"Ah, good morning," he said, in a voice like a TV announcer. "I wonder if you can help me. I'm looking into a claim from just over a year ago. A minor traffic accident that happened locally. In my paperwork here I see that one of your employees was a witness to the accident."

There was a moment's quiet as the other person was speaking.

"No, your vehicle wasn't involved at all. It's just that your employee was there and saw what happened and gave his name and that of the company."

I could hear, distantly, the voice on the other end of the phone.

"No, we never did need to contact him or you because the accident claim was settled without any problem. If only they were all as smooth as that! No, the reason I'm ringing is just to put the paperwork to bed, so to speak. Your employee signed his name but his writing is almost illegible and I wondered if you could just give me his name. It was in February, last year, round about Valentine's Day."

There was a silence and I felt my hands clench and unclench as I realized what Gerry was doing.

"Thanks, I'm really grateful. Here, I've just got my pad, I'll write the two names down. Right, right, is that Lea, L, E, A? No, it doesn't look like that's the name, what about the other one? Could you spell it out? That's it, that's the one! I'll be able to close this paperwork now. Thanks for your help."

I could still hear the other person speaking.

"Yes, I blame the schools, too. What on earth are they teaching them if they can't even sign their names clearly? Thanks again!"

He put the phone down and looked at me with a mischievous smile.

"They had two boys working for them at that time. One of them was Simon Lea and the other was a boy called Ian Payne, P, A, Y, N, E not P, A, I, N."

Ian Payne. The sandwich boy. The young man who worked in his father's café along the waterside. He had met both girls in the dentist's while he'd been selling sandwiches.

"Gerry, I feel like I could kiss you!" I said.

Gerry stood back slightly, as though afraid that I might really do it. I didn't mind. All I could think of was Ian Payne. The company van, the young man who got to know both girls while they were in the dentist's waiting to have their teeth done.

The sandwich boy, Ian Payne, was the missing link.

# 20

# Arrested

Heather finally called for me about four o'clock, almost five hours after I'd phoned her. She pulled up in a saloon car as I was at my front door, waiting. I bounced down the path and got into the passenger seat, the energy that I'd been sitting on all afternoon struggling to get out.

"Sorry it's been so long, Patsy," she said, pulling back out into the traffic.

She was carefully dressed as usual. She had a short straight skirt and thick black tights and boots. On top she had a light mac. Her hair was flicking over the collar, looking thick and well cut. She was wearing tiny penny glasses that I hadn't seen before.

"I need them for long distances," she said, as if reading my mind. "Your sight deteriorates with age,

Patsy, that's the trouble."

"My sight deteriorated when I was eleven," I said, pushing my glasses up. "What's been happening?"

"Lots. As soon as you rang I got a couple of my senior officers to pull out the case files again. I also sent an officer down to *Capricorn Sandwiches* to check out stuff there. That's why it's taken most of the afternoon. After the Mike Crosby fiasco we wanted to have as much evidence and information at our fingertips as we could. We've found out quite a lot."

"You think he did talk to the girls then, maybe offer them a lift when they came out of the dentist's?"

"That end of it is too speculative. We can't really know about that until we speak to Ian Payne. We've found out one or two other things, though."

"Can you tell me?" I said, noticing specks of rain on the windscreen.

She nodded her head and clicked on her wipers. "The sandwich company is a smallish catering firm based in Walthamstow. Their base is in one of the industrial units off the North Circular road. It's all small stuff down there: a manager, three or four women making the sandwiches and two delivery vans. A part of the workshop is leased out to two women who make fancy chocolates that go to the big department stores."

"Um…" I said, wondering why she was going into so much detail.

"When my officer went down there, he found this stuff all over the place." Heather reached over into the back seat and picked up some pink ribbon. I took it from her and let it sit in my hand. "They use it to gift-wrap the chocolates. Course you can buy the stuff in any wholesale catering place but…"

"Ian Payne could have got it from there."

"The other thing is that the boss there has a database on which he files everything to do with his staff. He was able to show us that Ian Payne didn't turn up for work on February fifteenth, sixteenth and seventeenth last year. Said he was looking after his dad who was ill. Not only that but on March fifteenth, the day that Jennifer Ryan's body was found, he didn't go into work and in fact never returned at all."

It was raining heavily by then and the traffic had slowed down. From outside the car I could hear the splashing of wheels going through puddles. I pictured Ian Payne, the non-communicative kid who worked behind the counter of the café. Was it really him who had pushed me into the river that night?

"The trouble is that Ian Payne was someone who we just never considered," Heather said. "At the time of the murders there was no mobile café there. He wasn't a part of the Scene."

"The café only opened in the summer."

"Right. But Ian Payne lives with his dad in a

house about a mile away from the river. That's probably why his dad decided to buy the site for the mobile café. It was close to home, a handy little business. Maybe the older Payne knew something and wanted to have his son working with him, to keep his eye on him."

"No, honestly, I don't think he could have known anything. He seems like a really nice man."

"In my experience parents will do almost anything to save their own children."

She was right, I knew.

"Anyway, we got in touch with the pub owner, Robert something something. We went over the list of people who he said were in the pub on the night that Jennifer was murdered. You might remember it was part of the bundle of stuff I gave you."

I nodded.

"OK, well, on that night he'd listed a group of locals and some passing trade, non-regulars who drop in and move on. When my officer spoke to him this afternoon he told us the same list of names but he also added that of Ian Payne."

"Why didn't he say that eighteen months ago, when he was first asked?" I said.

"Because, he said, at that time Payne wasn't a regular. At the time he hadn't known him from Adam. But now, now that he knows him from the stall, he is able to say that he *was* in the pub that night!"

"Did he say whether Ian was talking to Jennifer Ryan?"

"That was as much as we could get out of him. Not the most cooperative of men. We also found out that Ian Payne has been in trouble before. When he was fourteen he hit out at a girl in one of his classes at school. The girl was badly bruised and shaken up and he was arrested. The school persuaded the girl's parents to drop the charges, though. It seemed that Ian's mother had left home and a very messy divorce had taken place. The boy was pretty traumatized by it all."

We were nearing the river. The traffic was slow, though, and we were inching along, watching the rain skidding along the car windows. Eventually, we turned off the road and into the car park that backed on to the pub. Another car was there with two people sitting in it. I recognized one of them as an officer who Heather worked with.

The handbrake groaned loudly as Heather drew the car to a complete halt.

"We're going to do this low key and ask Ian to come down to the station with us voluntarily. If he doesn't I'll have to arrest him. I'm hoping we can avoid that because sometimes it leads to dramatics."

She opened the car door but then turned to me and said, "Whatever happens, Patsy, you keep out of it. You're a civilian here, you've no rights or powers to intervene."

I left my rucksack in the car and went out into the rain. It was five forty-five but the dark, solid clouds made it seem later. I zipped up my jacket and felt the rain peck at my skin. I followed Heather and the other two officers through the car park and round the side of the pub to the river walk.

The café was just up ahead, brightly lit against the grey brick walls of the disused factories and out-buildings. I could see Ian Payne behind the counter talking to two men who were standing under the canopy holding white cups of something, their rods and fishing gear at their feet. A gang of kids were standing around a few metres away, teenagers they looked like, hanging around in the rain with nothing to do. One of them looked round and evidently didn't like the look of the approaching adults. The group seemed to disintegrate as they wandered off in pairs. There's something obvious about the police, I guess, even when they're in plainclothes.

I felt nervous, I can't deny it. I'd never been on an actual arrest before. Even though part of me was revelling in the jubilation of finding a link and a suspect, there was another more cautionary voice whispering in my ear, "Don't be too confident, you've been wrong before…"

"Ian Payne? I'm Detective Inspector Heather Warren and these are Detectives Hutton and Clarke. I believe you've met our consultant, Patsy Kelly, before. There've been a number of developments in a case that we're looking into at the moment and your name has come up. I wonder if you wouldn't mind accompanying us to the station for a chat."

The men with the fishing gear had moved discreetly away from the cabin. Ian Payne was looking puzzled. Then worried. His dad wasn't around.

"What do you mean? What case? I don't know what you mean."

"It's probably better if we don't discuss it here in the open. I'm sure we can clear the whole thing up in just a few minutes down at the station."

"The *police* station?" Ian Payne said, as if we might have been asking him to accompany us to the train station. I looked behind Ian at the cabin walls. A complete wall chart of horoscopes sat in the middle of pin-ups of pop singers, boxers and soap stars. It had pride of place, yet I hadn't noticed that before.

"Just for a short while, sir," one of the officers said, giving Ian Payne the kind of smile a Lottery winner might expect. Outside the canopy, the rain was chucking down.

"I've got the café to look after. I can't just leave it."

"Is your father not around?"

"He'll be back any minute. I can't leave it unattended."

Just then the sound of a car door slamming came from somewhere behind the cabin. Alan Payne appeared a moment or two later with his hood up. He was carrying plastic bags of food just as he had been the first day I ever saw him.

"What's going on?" he said, looking at his son and then at Heather and the others. His eye fell on me. "Patsy Kelly, isn't it? What's happening here?"

Heather spoke immediately and gave Alan Payne the same information that she'd given his son.

"I don't understand, what case? You can't just say you're going to take him off."

"The river Lea murders, Mr Payne. We have reason to believe that Ian may have some information about the murders of Susan Yorke and Jennifer Ryan last year."

Alan Payne wore a puzzled expression, then, when the penny had finally dropped, he looked crestfallen. He looked at his son slowly and then at me.

"We have two choices. Either Ian comes quietly with us or we can charge him here and now. That seems to us to be unnecessary and public, Mr Payne."

Ian Payne hadn't said a word the whole time, his face a blank page.

Alan Payne was still looking around at everyone. Eventually he said, "Ian'll go with you, of course, until this stupid mess is sorted out. I'll close up the café. I'll come."

"Myself and Detective Hutton will take Ian into

custody, Mr Payne. Detective Clarke will give you a lift down to the station. That way we can go ahead."

"Thanks," Alan Payne said, his hands still full of the plastic bags of food.

"What about you, Patsy?" Heather said.

"I'll wait, I think. I can come along in the second car with Mr Payne," I said and watched the three of them walk out into the rain towards the car park, Ian Payne in the middle.

The truth was I felt sorry for Alan Payne, who still looked stunned as he went into the cabin and turned off the hot plates and put away the cooking implements. He held up a plate of cakes and offered them to us in a kind of dazed way. "I don't want no money for them," he said in explanation, but we both shook our heads and he put them into a Tupperware box.

"I won't be long," he said, "only I need to pack up properly. What with the café being out here, un-attended all night, everything has to be under lock and key. That way it'll be all right when we start up tomorrow."

I looked at Detective Clarke who was tapping his foot and glancing from time to time at his watch.

"Otherwise we get wild animals in here, foxes and the like. I'll just put this stuff in the freezer." He was opening and closing doors, moving things from one surface to the other. It didn't look like there was much organization: he was just keeping busy.

"We ought to be going," the officer said, with a quick smile.

"Right, I'll get my keys."

Alan Payne got a plastic box from under the counter and tipped it out. There were at least half a dozen small padlocks. I noticed his hands were shaking and he kept looking at the police officer and then back to me. He was upset. His son would likely be arrested for two unpleasant murders. He was in shock.

Detective Clarke drew a long breath of exasperation which Alan Payne didn't seem to notice.

"Why don't you go on?" I said to him. "I'll wait and go with Mr Payne in his own car."

"Are you sure?" he said, holding his hand out from under the canopy to see if it was still raining.

"Yes, I'm not rushing anywhere. We'll probably be down the station in about thirty minutes. You go on."

"If you're sure," he said, turning to go even before the words were out.

"See you later," I shouted, watching him walk up the path in the failing light, his footsteps sounding and then fading away.

"I'm really sorry about Ian," I said, turning back to Alan Payne.

"There's no need!" he said buoyantly. "My Ian is innocent. There's been a mistake. As soon as it's all cleared up he'll be back here working beside me again. My Ian wouldn't hurt a fly."

I didn't answer. I just waited for him to attach all the padlocks and then slowly come out of the cabin, locking and double-locking the doors. In his hand was a bottle of cooking oil and the Tupperware box of cakes.

"Van's round here," he said, leading the way behind the cabin and into an alley that I hadn't seen before. Just as I was about to go I heard a siren from the main road, its sound distant, yet comforting. Another followed it and I wondered what was happening.

Alan Payne walked ahead to a tiny cul-de-sac. It looked like it used to be the entrance for one of the riverside factories. Now it was desolate, the big iron gates to the factory padlocked and security notices all over the wire.

"We always park the van here," he said. "It's the quickest way to the café. Not many people use it. It's off the beaten track."

Nobody was using it. It was just the two of us surrounded by grey brick walls, empty buildings, barbed wire and broken windows. A solitary black cat was walking across the road, its steps slow and deliberate, its head lowered as though it was preying on something.

"I'll just put this stuff in the back of the van," Alan Payne said and got his keys out. I waited by the passenger door and I heard him groan.

"What's the matter?" I said.

"Oh, no," was all I heard.

I walked round the back of the van. Alan Payne was looking glumly inside it.

"What's up, have you been broken into?"

I turned to look into the back of the van. All I could see was a couple of cardboard boxes and some trays of canned drinks. Nothing else.

"What's happened?" I said.

There was no answer and I was about to turn round when I heard this thud and felt an intense pressure on the back of my head, as if I'd been hit by a bowling ball.

Then everything went black.

# 21
# Caught

When I opened my eyes I was lying in the dark with my hands tied up behind me. The back of my head felt as though it had a heavy weight on it and somewhere behind my eyes there was a ball of pain. My shoulders were stiff and I began to move about. It was then that I realized I was lying on the floor of the van. I began to wiggle my wrists about, trying to free my hands. They were fastened tightly and after a few seconds I stopped and felt the ties with my fingers. It was the ribbon that the other girls had been tied up with. Even though I couldn't see it I imagined it wound round and round my wrists, pink and shiny, the ends hanging in loose curls.

I managed to sit up a bit, pushing myself against

a cardboard box. I looked around the small space I was in, just wide enough for me to stretch out my legs. The doors at the other end were closed and I kicked out at them two, three times but they didn't budge. The partition between the back of the van and the driver's seat was closed over.

I was in a black box, my hands tied, waiting for Alan Payne to come back and kill me the way he had killed the others. I shouted out, loud as I could, but my own voice echoed in the tiny van and I knew that there was very little likelihood of anyone hearing me.

My throat felt like I had just swallowed razor blades and my eyes filled with water. I pulled my hands against the ties but they didn't budge and I felt the pretty ribbon digging into my skin like cheese-wire.

Alan Payne had killed the two girls, not his son, Ian. Why, because they had been horrible to his son? Because he had wanted them and they had rejected him? Had they met him in the dentist's as I'd thought? He'd given them a lift, perhaps, got friendly, seen them again, met them, offered lifts, friendship, more, much more. Neither of them had wanted him. Susan had very likely told him to get lost. Jennifer had let him drive her round and then dumped him when she was fed up.

It had been Alan, his father, who had pushed me into the river; he who had hung around outside St

Michael's hostel and taken a photograph of me. It had been Alan Payne who had sent me a note saying PATSY KELLY. DEATH BY DROWNING. YOU'RE NEXT.

I lay on my side, my knees up to my chest and battled against the panic that was gathering inside. How long, I kept asking myself, how long, until he comes back for me.

It seemed like hours but I knew it wasn't as long as that. I couldn't look at my watch so I ended up trying to count in my head to keep calm. When I got to six hundred and something I lost count and started again. In the middle of the first hundred he came back.

I heard footsteps along the pavement and then the sound of the driver's door being opened.

"Hello?" I said, but there was no answer. The right side of the van creaked and lowered and then there was the sound of the ignition key being turned.

"Hello? Mr Payne? Alan? Is that you?"

"Yes, Patsy, it's me. We're just going for a drive. You be a good girl now."

Even though I expected him to speak, his voice was a shock. His tone was light-hearted as though I was a child and he'd just left me in the car while he got a bit of shopping. I'd expected a sneer, some anger, something uncontrolled. Somehow it was worse, to be spoken to as though everything was right with the world when I knew that I was in the worst trouble that I'd ever been in.

The van started off and seemed to be inching forward slowly as if we were going over an uneven road or waste ground. There were still no sounds from outside, no traffic, nothing. I knew then that he was taking me further along the river. I pushed myself up and moved across the floor until my back was against the doors. It was as if I was getting as much space between us as I could. The doors behind me were firmly closed and all I could see was the back of Alan Payne's head.

I thought about my mum at home and felt this terrible sense of loss, as though it was she who was in danger, not me. Then I pictured Billy, my boy-friend, spending the day working on his new job, blithely unaware of what was happening.

I started to beg.

"Alan, please, this is silly. The police will know. If you hurt me they'll know it was you. You're bound to get caught. What's the point?"

He turned his head very slightly.

"No, Patsy. See, I've just been down to the police station and reported in. I told them I'd given you a lift home. Ian's waiting for a solicitor so I said I'd go and change, have something to eat then get back there. It'll be a long time before anyone misses you, Patsy, and by that time it'll be too late."

The van was slowing down and I felt this torrent of panic that made it difficult for me to breathe.

"But why? I've done nothing to you or your son."

"That's true enough. You're not in the same class as those other two tramps! They thought they'd use my son for their own ends, then drop him when he wasn't required. They took on more than they bargained for. See, I know what trouble women can be. I know how they can use a man up then discard him when they've had enough or when they find someone new. No, you're different, Patsy. You're just convenient. See, if my son's in custody and another young girl's body is found, how can it be him who did the rest?"

"But they'll know it was you!"

"Why? Why on earth should they think that? They've no reason to. They'll be very apologetic, Patsy, for falsely arresting my son."

I couldn't answer. His calmness was cutting into me and a feeling of nausea was swirling about my stomach. I wanted to be sick but didn't have the strength. I made myself keep on speaking. Anything to fill the awful silence and the sound of the van on the uneven ground underneath.

"You brought both of them here, like this?" I said. "In the van, to this spot?"

"That's right."

"But you didn't hit them on the head?"

"No, a small knife and a few threats kept them quiet, got them into the van."

"But there weren't any bruises, no signs of trying to escape," I said dully.

"No. They thought I was just going to teach them a lesson. I told them I was taking them for a ride and that I was just going to tell them what I thought of them. I told them if they were good girls and didn't make any trouble for me I would take them back to the road and let them off."

"And they believed you?"

"They wanted to believe me. Both of them, they were desperate to believe me."

The van came to a stop and I closed my eyes, thinking of Susan and Jennifer, lying wide-eyed in the back of the van, their hands tied behind their backs, fervently wanting to believe that he was going to let them go.

"But Jennifer wouldn't have believed you. She must have known about the first girl."

"The homeless kid? No. It was in the paper for a couple of days and then it disappeared. Nobody knew about it until the second one was found." Alan Payne turned round and faced me for the first time. "I was there that day, standing among the crowd. I watched as they pulled her up out of the water. That was the very day I saw the billboard for the café site. *Leasehold For Sale*, it said. It wasn't a part of the river that I frequented much. If it hadn't been for the body floating up I'd not have noticed the sign. And I was right. It was a perfect place for me and Ian to set up business."

He opened his door and I knew he was going to get out and walk round to the back. There were only moments left, I knew, before he would come and lead me out of the van and towards the river. Once I was there I had no chance at all. He was heavier than me, stronger than me and he had his hands free. I was finished.

I turned my body round so that I was facing the doors, took several deep breaths and waited for him to open them.

A couple of clicks and the night air rushed in. He was standing, a metre or so back, his arms folded and the beginnings of a smile on his face. I pulled all my courage together and got out of the van.

"Please, Alan," I said, "I won't do anything, I promise. I won't tell a soul."

He was in charge and began to shake his head. I stood, just a short way away from him, my hands pulled behind me, making it hard to keep my balance.

"Don't make this harder for yourself, Patsy, there's a good girl."

He said it in a jovial way and moved his arms in my direction. I walked closer to him, into his arms, taking what were the most difficult steps of my life.

"There's a good girl," he said, putting a hand on each of my shoulders.

I got as close as possible to him and inside my head I counted to three. Then I brought my knee up between his legs as hard as I could.

He stepped back in shock, his hands shooting down to cover himself, his voice escaping with pain. That's when I lifted my leg again, aimed for his groin and kicked out as hard as I could.

Then I turned and ran, taking giant strides in the dark away from the van, up the uneven path and towards some distant lighting.

I didn't stop to listen or look to see if he had got up and was running after me, I just kept running, faster than I've ever run in my life, my hands held uselessly behind my back, tensing myself in case I lost my footing and fell straight on to my face. After a few minutes I came to a gate and ran through it on to an empty road that led past some of the old disused factories. I took a right turn away from the river and kept going, the blood pulsing through my head, the ribbon eating into my wrists. Up ahead there were some streetlights and I ran in the direction of them, my breath tearing in and out of my lungs.

From behind me I heard the van. Amid the quiet of the streets the soft purr of the engine sounded in my head. Up in front was the streetlight, some cars passing by. If I could just keep running, if I could just get to the road...

I turned a corner and found myself in an alley that led between two of the old factories. It was dark, but not so dark that I couldn't see where I was going. From far behind me I heard the brakes of the van and a door slamming and I knew that Alan Payne had got out and was on foot after me. I ran blindly to the end of the alley, not knowing what was waiting for me. When I got there I looked with dismay at the river.

I turned round and saw him there, walking towards me, a smile on his face.

I thought that was the end. I almost stopped and gave up. I had no breath left and for one wild moment I felt as if I was already under the black water, surrounded by silence and feeling the heavy pull of the river bed.

A single peal of laughter rang out and I looked to the right and saw, in the distance, the lights of the Willow Tree glittering. With every bit of strength I had, I turned and ran, only a step away from the river, past the barges and under the dark bridge, past the café and into the garden, zigzagging through the empty tables and chairs until I burst through the doors of the saloon bar.

Inside, behind the bar, was Robert Pettiford Wilson, cleaning a glass, looking at me as though I was an alien from another planet.

It was then that I noticed that the pain in my head was as big as a football.

"Help me," I said, "please, please help me."

An ambulance took me to the local hospital while the police scoured the area for Alan Payne. They used tracker dogs as well as cars and a helicopter with heat–seeking equipment. They didn't find him.

The next morning he gave himself up at the local police station.

# 22

# Neat Endings

After I got out of hospital, I spent a day in the office typing up the report and then arranged to go up to Kerry Yorke's. I'd asked her if I could bring Tanya with me. Billy drove us there.

Billy had, in fact, spent just about every waking moment with me. In the office he'd made cups of tea and done errands, often getting in my uncle Tony's way. In my house he'd made me sandwiches and found me the newspapers and the remote control and kept saying, "Is there anything you want?" and then sitting about a centimetre away from me while I watched as much daytime TV as I could stand.

On the way to Kerry Yorke's, Tanya sat in the back of the car. By her side, on the seat, was Tiggy, his head on her lap and his big marble eyes looking from me to Tanya and back again. She was reading the local newspaper which had all the details about the case.

"It says, COLD-BLOODED KILLER FOILED BY KID DETECTIVE," she said, reading the headline slowly and loudly as if it had great importance.

"I know," I said. I'd already read the article and phoned up the reporter to complain about the head-line.

"It goes on," she said, "Alan Payne split up with his wife of fifteen years after a bitter break-up which involved another man. Tina Payne, a thirty-nine-year-old petite blonde, said, 'Alan was never violent with me but I always thought he was capable of it. He turned my son against me and never gave me a penny out of the divorce settlement.'"

"Is that why they think he did it? Because of the way his wife treated him?" Billy said, an incred-ulous tone in his voice.

I shrugged my shoulders. I didn't know. To tell the truth, the whole subject gave me the creeps every time I thought about it. Alan Payne, the nice man who ran the café, the father that I'd felt sorry for. Instead he'd been cold-blooded and ruthless and would have cast me into the river like a used sweet wrapper.

I wanted to distance myself from the case. I was

looking forward to dropping Tanya off at Kerry Yorke's, giving her the report and saying my good-byes.

"What about Ian? Did he know?" Billy said, his hand stretching across and touching my arm fleetingly.

"I don't think so."

"Didn't he think it was a bit odd, though? He gets involved with two girls and then they both end up dead. It wouldn't take a genius to work out some connection there."

"That's true," I said. "It seems, though, that Ian knew nothing. He says that after the bodies had been found he talked to his dad about going to the police to say that he'd been friendly with the girls. His dad had advised against it, though. Alan Payne warned Ian that it would look like he had done it and as the police were desperate for a conviction he would be the most obvious one."

"So Ian kept his mouth shut."

"He said he thought his link was irrelevant because he knew that it hadn't been him."

"So he just kept quiet," Tanya said, joining in.

"Yes," I said.

We were coming up to Woodford and Tanya started to look a bit uncomfortable.

"What's Susie's mum like?" she said, giving Tiggy a hug.

"She's nice. Really warm, says what she means."

"Why's she want to see me?"

"Because you spent time with Susan before she died. She wants to talk to you about Susan."

"She's not expecting me to stay the night, is she? I've got to get back to the hostel. I've got people to see and stuff to do."

"No. We'll make sure you get back to the hostel for six-thirty."

I meant it. Deep down inside, though, I had this fairy-tale hope that Kerry would like Tanya and Tanya would like Kerry. Maybe not all at once, not even overnight. But I kept thinking, what if they kept in touch? Became friends? Kerry could help Tanya, find her a place to live. Tanya could be a comfort to Kerry. It seemed so simple. Tanya had no mother and Kerry had no daughter. Why couldn't they be together?

But Billy had told me to be realistic. You can't just replace people with other people. In real life it didn't work like that.

Kerry Yorke was at her front gate as we drove up. She had black leather trousers on and her scraggy blonde hair was flying in all directions. She had a T-shirt that said LIFE'S A LOTTERY and I couldn't help smiling looking at her. When I got out of the car she came straight across and gave me a hug. Over her shoulder, I could see an older woman from the house next door peeking out to see what was happening.

"Didn't I say you were a smart kid?" Kerry Yorke said, a wide smile on her face.

Tanya got out, her red hair frizzed out around her face. Tiggy jumped out behind her and promptly cocked his leg up against Kerry's garden wall.

"Kerry, this is Tanya, who I told you about, and this is my boyfriend, Billy."

"Come in, come in," Kerry said, delightedly, "we don't want the neighbours talking."

We dropped Tanya off at the hostel later that afternoon. Then we went back to my house.

"I liked Kerry Yorke," Billy said. "I think it was really generous of her to give so much money to the hostel."

Two hundred thousand pounds. It was a lot of money, even to a millionaire. St Michael's would now be able to do expensive refurbishments and build a special day room so that the clients wouldn't be chucked out on to the street every morning.

It wouldn't affect Peter Lee, though. He had resigned, along with Mike Crosby. Both of them disgraced. Big Alice was temporarily in charge of the hostel.

As we drove along there was a lengthening silence as though Billy was building himself up to saying something. It was probably about his new job. He'd kept it all in since the night he'd told me in his candle-lit kitchen. I had a feeling his words had multiplied inside him and were desperately trying to come out.

"Are you thinking about your new job?" I said, quietly.

"I don't know what to do about it, Patsy," he said, finally.

"What do you mean?"

"I'm not so sure now it's the right thing to do."

He had been very sure during the time that he'd applied for it, gone for the interviews, built himself up to tell me. But the events of the past week had thrown him, I was sure. Instead of being his reliable girlfriend, I had almost turned into his dead girl-friend. It had scrambled all his plans.

"When have you got to make up your mind?"

"There are several training sessions," he said, "but we don't actually go for about eight weeks."

"Plenty of time. Don't make any decisions now. Just see how you feel in a couple of weeks."

He didn't answer. I actually thought he should go to Africa. I knew that it would be the right thing for him to do. What would it mean for us as a couple? I wasn't sure, but we'd been close for a long time and I began to think that another year might not make a bit of difference.

When we arrived at my house I went straight through into the kitchen. My mum and Gerry were sitting side by side, their arms linked, their faces round and smiley. Billy came in behind me and we both stood looking at them. On the table was an unopened bottle of champagne and four glasses.

There was also this air of expectancy, a hidden secret, a bit of news waiting to burst out.

My mum was the first to speak.

"Guess what, Patsy!"

"Let me see now." I looked at the champagne and then back to the pair of them. "Could it be that you and Gerry are going to get married?"

"Now, how did you know that?" she said mischievously.

"You can't keep anything from me," I said. "I'm a detective."

# P●INT CRiME

# THE EAST END MURDERS

## It's a capital offence not to read them.

**A Family Affair**
The body of a young girl, soaked in petrol and
abandoned in a derelict house...

**End of the Line**
Four victims in ten days. But is the *Railway
Killer* still at large?

**No Through Road**
Dead – and encased in concrete...

**Accidental Death**
When your best friend is arrested, you have to
do *something*...

**Brotherly Love**
A witness is a dangerous thing to be...

**Death By Drowning**
Investigation can be dangerous – or even fatal...

**Killing Time**
Accident or suicide? Or maybe murder...

*Anne Cassidy*

# Point Horror Unleashed

**Point Horror Unleashed.**
**It's one step beyond...**

# Confessions

Difficult decisions.
Dangerous mistakes.
It's what life's all about…

## He Loved Drugs More Than Me
## My Sister – The Superbitch
Rosie Corrigan

## I Slept With My Best Friend's Boyfriend
## I Abandoned My Baby
Sue Dando

## My Boyfriend's Older Than My Dad
Jill Eckersley

## They Think I'm Too Easy…
Lorna Read

## I Taught Him A Lesson He'll Never Forget
Amber Vane

## Will He Love Me If I'm Thin?
Kirsty White